Even the gray Paris skies seemed to mourn the duchess

A thin misty drizzle drifted up from the Seine as the four men slid the coffin from its carrier.

Alexei Kirov signaled the others to lift the wooden casket to their shoulders. Mack Bolan walked opposite Kirov at the head of the procession.

They lowered the case into the hole and the priest finished his final blessing. Kirov scattered a handful of damp earth onto the casket's cover.

As Bolan bent forward to do the same, he felt an explosive impact slam between his shoulder blades with excruciating force.

He pitched headfirst into the open grave.

MACK BOLAN

The Executioner

DON PENDLETON's EXECUTIONER
MACK BOLAN
Hammerhead Reef

A GOLD EAGLE BOOK FROM
WØRLDWIDE

TORONTO • NEW YORK • LONDON • PARIS
AMSTERDAM • STOCKHOLM • HAMBURG
ATHENS • MILAN • TOKYO • SYDNEY

First edition October 1985

ISBN 0-373-61082-3

Special thanks and acknowledgment to
Alan Bomack for his contributions to this work.

To the memory of U.S. Army Major Arthur Nicholson,
shot to death by a Soviet sentry
in northern East Germany in March, 1985.

All the great struggles of history have been won
by superior willpower wresting victory in the teeth of
odds or upon the narrowest of margins.

—Winston Churchill

I live by the hour. Each new day I see is an unexpected
victory. Whether I'll live another day or drown in my
own blood an hour from now is not the greatest worry
of my life. But I have to fight my war my way.

—Mack Bolan

Prologue

IDENTIFY...

Mack Bolan's right hand rested lightly on the special M-39 that lay on the seat beside him. The Executioner had chosen a new weapon for this probe. The Smith & Wesson pistol was highly modified for combat. And Alphabet Town was a combat zone.

Bolan expected trouble.

And he was ready for it.

The drunk staggered slowly toward Bolan's rental car. The wino's shabby pea jacket was spotted with stale vomit. One arm wavered uncertainly in a half circle, then, after pausing to regain his balance, he shuffled off at an angle across the nearby vacant lot.

Bolan dismissed the man and resumed surveillance of the maroon Mercedes parked fifty yards ahead on Avenue D. The drunk was no more than he appeared to be—just another miserable bum on the Lower East Side—but Bolan's caution was well-founded. He knew in these parts an unsuspecting citizen could get his throat slit for less than the price of a joint.

Anybody, no matter what their status or age—and minors were especially welcome prey—could get anything they wanted, so long as they had the money. From amphetamines of every stripe to Zach's Seventh Heaven, a potent brand of heroin, Alphabet Town was a lexicon of chemical evil.

Bolan knew the man behind the wheel of the German luxury car. The driver was Art Brewster, PR man for Funkytown Records.

The Executioner watched as Brewster powered down the window of the Mercedes and leaned across the seat. He was probably looking to score a supply of A Train high-grade and enough cocaine to mix up the speedballs that would fry his brain for the weekend.

The pusher walked nonchalantly toward the elegant car.

The deal was going down.

Bolan double-checked to make sure that the M-39 was fully loaded, and slipped it into an armpit holster just as a squad car from the Ninth Precinct cruised past. The two young officers were sharing a private joke, glancing only occasionally at the action on the street.

Bolan climbed out from behind the wheel. He saw two rats scurrying away from the pile of garbage against the tenement wall. And the soldier couldn't help thinking that the real vermin were walking the streets.

Bolan hovered in the shadows of an alleyway, fighting an urge to leave this place and take a shower. The place stank of rot and filth and corruption.

Art Brewster handed over a folded wad of bills. The courier flipped through the notes with a practiced thumb before giving the Funkytown executive the package of dream powders he craved so badly.

Bolan seethed with a strangely troubled anger. He had executed pushers before, but what do you do when the target is an eight-year-old boy?

He had been carrying the drug supply in a plastic lunch box. Bolan followed the youngster as he walked off with a swagger well beyond his years.

The Mercedes pulled a U-turn through a break in the traffic. Bolan did not turn to watch the car go. Brewster was strictly small fry. There were bigger fish to snag.

Much bigger.

Art Brewster was just another overreaching loser.

Bolan knew he couldn't stop every trendy business-man who wanted to freebase. He couldn't read the riot act to every misguided teenager who wanted to smoke pot. If they were intent on poisoning their bodies and polluting their minds that was their business—at least, that's the first line of defense of every drug user.

Freedom of choice, sure.

No way.

It was not simply that Bolan had far more respect for his own physical and mental well-being, but he was only too aware of the broader picture.

Every time a white-collar worker or a chic hairdresser snorted a line of coke, they condoned a cop on the take or a gang war in Miami.

Each time a magazine editor or a rich kid from Long Island booted heroin, they were distant accessories to a stabbing in Houston. When a couple of college fresh-men shared a joint, they agreed to a contract killing in Louisiana.

And a long-haired record executive had just encour-aged a young boy—a third-grader at that—to pursue a life of crime.

Each user on a high might have thought he was king of the heap. But they were all just low men on the totem pole. The grim-faced Executioner wanted the chiefs. And they had to be hit where it hurt.

The boy reached up to high-five a black dude in a red beret, skipped around a group of street dancers, then ran toward a well-dressed Hispanic lounging against the plate-glass window of a delicatessen.

Bolan pedigreed the "entrepreneur." His name was Paco Quesada.

The Executioner saw Quesada pat the kid's unruly hair. Then the errand boy handed over the brightly colored lunch pail.

Another squad car drifted past.

Bolan waited.

ISOLATE...

The trail led back to Jackson Heights.

Paco Quesada made two more collections from his team of underaged hustlers, placed a phone call, then got into his Firebird and drove across the Williamsburg Bridge.

Bolan followed in the rented Chevy.

Quesada left the expressway at Queens Boulevard and swung north again to Roosevelt. The streetlights were starting to flicker on as the two cars entered the Hispanic district of Jackson Heights.

Quesada stopped at the Restaurante Rincón, an eatery owned by Gabriel Ojeda. He and Quesada were accompanied by Ricardo Lopez, a man with dark piercing eyes that were ever watchful. Lopez was a "soldier," newly imported from Bogotá to serve the Ojeda family.

Still Bolan waited...mentally recording each new face, each new contact, assessing their capabilities and probable rank in the complex hierarchy of the Colombian gang world.

The men lingered on the sidewalk saying farewell. Quesada's hand brushed Ricardo's forearm. The bodyguard drew back. He did not like to be touched.

Finally the sleek Firebird led Bolan to a side street off Roosevelt. Quesada walked over to the doorway next to a dry cleaners and pushed the buzzer. He tried a second time and stepped back out onto the sidewalk.

"HIJO DE PUTA!" Raoul Silva swore when he heard the sound of his apartment's buzzer. He slipped the rolled-up ten-dollar note into his pocket, then quickly used his index finger to scrape the line of white powder off the table into the small plastic bag.

He was concealing the bag of cocaine behind some frozen food in the freezer compartment of his fridge when the buzzer sounded again.

Raoul rushed to the window and poked his head out. He casually fingered the small gold crucifix on the chain around his neck and, as he looked down, saw Paco Quesada on the sidewalk below.

"Hey, Raoul, *ese. Qué tal, hombre.* It's your old *amigo*, Paco."

Raoul was annoyed—and jittery. He needed a hit bad.

And he was not in a sociable mood. Especially since his *tiempo del sueño*—his "dreamtime" as he called it—had been so rudely interrupted.

Besides, Paco was not an old friend.

He was a contact Raoul had been given before he left Barranquilla. But anyone who could give the young Colombian an occasional night's work at five thousand dollars a shot could call himself anything he wanted.

"You bring word from Ojeda?"

"*Si*, Raoul, don't I always? But not out here."

Silva pushed his fingers through his lips and blew a hungry whistle at the girl hurrying down to pick up some overtime at the garment factory. She tossed her head in a token show of disapproval. But Silva had already ducked back inside to let Quesada into his modest apartment.

Raoul was being very careful with the money he was making as a swimmer for the Ojeda clan. He was saving every cent he could to marry Miranda, the youngest daughter of the lawyer Luis Escobar.

Raoul had never even spoken to her, but he'd seen her many times. In Barranquilla they did not move in the same circles. A waterfront brat like Silva was completely beneath the wealthy Escobars. But it would be different when he went back with a suitcase full of *yanqui* dollars. The money would smooth out any difference in their social strata. Raoul was sure of it.

Bolan watched as Quesada disappeared into the building.

If he had been truly careful, Silva would have taken a long, hard second look at the shadowy figure behind the tinted glass in the Chevy parked down the street. But the flamboyant Hispanic did not expect Death to call on him so soon.

The two men were mere cogs in the machine that converted the leaves of the coca plant from the northern Andes into billions of greenbacks for the crime families who now lived in this quiet residential district of New York.

Bolan meant to destroy that machine.

In time.

The fuse was lit and burning dangerously low. But Bolan's anger was controlled, focused. It did not interfere with his patience.

Long nights of waiting for the enemy in the Asian jungles had taught the soldier that patience meant survival.

It was a different jungle this time. But the enemy was no less savage.

Patience, the warrior knew, was as important to a sniper as marksmanship.

And Bolan was very good at both.

But the waiting would soon be over.

He could feel it.

...DESTROY!

An hour later, Paco Quesada left Raoul Silva's apartment and headed back toward Alphabet Town. Bolan was about to follow him when a second car pulled up outside Silva's inconspicuous apartment. The Colombian must have been ready and waiting. He appeared almost immediately, ran across the sidewalk and jumped into the beat-up Ford. He was carrying a bulky Adidas sports tote.

Bolan hung back, keeping to the blind side, as the two men wheeled toward Brooklyn.

The Chevy was forced to stop by a fast-changing red and then had to slow down again as a large container truck backed out onto the road, but there wasn't enough traffic for Bolan to lose the quarry.

A tugboat hooted in the distance and the skeletal arms of the dockside cranes were silhouetted against the garish night-sky glow of Manhattan across the river.

And grim death was right on the tail of the battered Ford as it turned onto Atlantic Avenue.

Silva and his buddy slowed down. They were too intent on finding the right wharf to realize that a dark shadow had trailed them from Jackson Heights.

They circled twice past the *Santa Clara*, a rust-streaked freighter out of Panama, marking the ship for themselves and the ice-blue eyes of their unseen tracker.

Bolan pulled his car in behind a giant dumpster that partially blocked an alley opposite the dock gates. The narrow lane reeked of rotting garbage. Three berths down, the longshoremen were pulling a swing shift to unload cargo from a German vessel, but all was quiet aboard the *Santa Clara*.

The two Colombians made a third pass—for Gabriel Ojeda would permit them no mistakes, Bolan knew—and this time the Ford stopped. Raoul Silva jumped out. He was still carrying the bulging sports bag.

An old wooden shed squatted about thirty yards to the left of the locked gates. The nearest floodlight was broken.

Bolan suspected it had been put out of commission on Ojeda's instructions. Silva hurried for this darkened refuge by the storage locker.

After looking both ways along the street, Silva peeled back a section of the chain-link fence and pushed the bag through first.

The opening had no doubt been precut by the same man who had knocked out the light. As soon as Raoul Silva had safely wriggled through the fence, his friend pulled away.

The Executioner spent a moment wondering if the wheelman was going to park the Ford a couple of blocks away so as not to attract unwelcome attention. Or would he return after a specified time to pick up Silva?

No time for guessing games, the warrior decided. If he didn't make his move he would lose them both. He would stick with Raoul Silva. The diver was more important than the driver.

Bolan was dressed in combat black, but for once, his skintight suit was devoid of weapons, except for the M-39 and a stiletto strapped to his calf. Like a moving shadow in the gloom, he ran toward the spot where the young hood had disappeared.

The Executioner circled warily toward the edge of the wharf, then crouched beside the abandoned tote bag.

He heard the faint squeak of a little-used ladder protesting the Colombian's weight...then a slight ripple running counter to the gentle lapping of the water.

Gun in hand, the death stalker crept closer.

RAOUL SILVA FELT A SHIVER of apprehension and excitement as he slipped off his jeans and pulled on a wet suit.

He knew this was not going to be a leisurely swim. He would be down there just long enough to cut free the two five-kilo packs that had been sunk below the stern of the *Santa Clara*. From the bottom of the large sports bag he retrieved a waterproof flashlight, mask and a small twin-cylinder breathing apparatus.

He strapped on the diving equipment and eased his body into the murky water....

The moment Raoul broke the surface, he looked at his watch and nodded. Four minutes was all it had taken for him to collect the payload, the *Santa Clara*'s real cargo.

And five thousand dollars would be added to the money he needed to marry Miranda. Not bad for four minutes' work.

Now ten more keys of the finest Colombian cocaine would be cut to be snorted by rich *norteamericanos*.

With three powerful strokes Silva reached the bottom rung of the ladder. He paused there a moment, letting the diving knife dangle from its wrist strap as he pushed the mask up onto his forehead.

The river water stank, but what the hell, it was easy money! Silva felt pleased with himself as he lugged the two packages up the ladder.

The shadow of the Panamanian rust bucket bobbed gently behind him, a gloomy wall of riveted plating, as he put one arm over the splintered edge of the wharf and began to lever himself topside.

But another shadow loomed to his right, closer and even more menacing.

A man stood there, black against black, but not so dark that Silva could not see the outline of the gun.

The weapon was pointed directly at his head. He was staring right into its unforgiving eye.

"Push it over here, slimeball!" growled the voice.

Silva registered the ice-cold tone and realized he had no choice. He poked the two dripping packages forward.

"Now you...easy." The apparition in black signaled with his left hand. The gun barrel did not waver for an instant.

The diver climbed onto the wooden planks of the wharf. He shook his head to get rid of the water trickling into his eyes. He wanted a better look at the owner of the voice.

A sudden chill ran through him when the man spoke again.

"That's far enough. Drop the knife!"

Silva shrugged slightly as he raised his arm to show that the blade was still secured to his wrist.

"Shake it loose. I want to hear it drop."

Even in that ghostly half light Silva gave himself away. There was the suggestion of a smile curling at the corner of his mouth, and maybe a flicker of hope in those dark eyes. For a man who was only one mistake away from eternity, Silva looked suddenly confident.

Bolan's combat senses had already alerted him. Silva's buddy was back...and almost on top of them!

The smallest gasp of indrawn breath was the final signal as the man behind swung down with the cargo hook.

Bolan dropped to one knee and twisted rapidly to the side as the lethal point ripped through the fabric of his skinsuit. Then the man was on top of him, chopping savagely for a second time.

Bolan grabbed the attacker's wrist, letting the man's own momentum propel him over his shoulder. The hookman cartwheeled forward but the Executioner still held his arm in a rigid lock. Tendons tore apart and his shoulder separated as the driver slammed onto the pier.

Silva had flipped the knife into his grasp and came in with a sweeping cut. Never releasing his hold, Bolan swung the screaming body of the wheelman right in Silva's path. The razor-sharp point of the knife sank deeply into the abdomen of Bolan's attacker.

For a staggered heartbeat the two Colombians stood in a blood-drenched embrace.

"Amateurs," Bolan growled in disgust as he squeezed off the Smith & Wesson.

A lightning flash blasted the night. Silva's rib cage imploded jaggedly as he tottered back along the edge of the dock.

Bolan grabbed the crumpling corpse of the gut-slashed driver and shoved hard. The two men from Barranquilla collided for a second time, then together fell off the wharf.

The night warrior used his own knife to rip open the heavy plastic pouches. The white powder scattered like a poisonous cloud over the garbage-strewn waters below.

Who was Miranda, Bolan wondered. It was the last word uttered by the young swimmer as he fell from the dockside.

Bolan came out of the shower just as the phone rang.

With a towel draped over his shoulder he strode to the side table.

"Yes?" was his only answer.

"Mr. Bolan?"

The voice was as unmistakable as the vaguely hollow static of the long-distance connection. Alexei Kirov was one of the few people who knew how to reach Bolan directly. The Russian expatriate always sounded formal, but tonight there was a mournful edge to his voice.

"What is it, Alexei?" asked Bolan, although he had already guessed the probable reason for a late-night call from Marijana's retainer.

"The Grand Duchess—"

"When?"

"Last night, Mr. Bolan. Peacefully. In her sleep." Kirov sounded tired. Bolan glanced at the clock. It must have been nearly dawn in Paris. "I tried to get hold of you earlier this morning. I was sure you would want to know."

"Yes, thank you, Alexei." Bolan felt a pang of regret for not having seen Marijana again before it happened.

It was not the agonizing stab of pain he knew at the deaths of his family or of April Rose, but a profound sense of loss for a friend who had become his staunch supporter.

The Duchess Marijana had used her contacts to help him get inside Russia when he needed to clear his name of the Macek assassination.

And she had been of quiet but very real financial assistance since the Executioner had so forcefully severed ties with his government. Her funds had in large part fueled his new solo war against their common enemy—the Soviet death machine and its KGB controllers.

"The duchess lived a full life," summed up the American.

"She was indeed a great lady," replied Kirov. "The last of her kind."

Odd, but that was the very same sentiment the duchess had herself expressed to Bolan during their first meeting in Paris.

"There will be a small ceremony," said the Russian retainer, faithful to the end, "tomorrow afternoon at the church of Saint Bernard. I thought perhaps—"

"I'll be there, Alexei." Bolan would pay his last respects in person.

It was time to say farewell to yet another comrade-at-arms in the ceaseless war.

IT WAS MIDMORNING in Moscow, although it was difficult to tell the exact time of day from the dull gray light that filtered through the grimy windows of Strakhov's office.

The small suite that accommodated the Thirteenth Section was on the third floor of the KGB's baroque headquarters in Dzerzhinsky Square.

And from this well-guarded lair Maj. Gen. Greb Strakhov controlled an invisible army of assassins—the cold-eyed men who watched the watchers—which spread its terror tentacles around the world.

Strakhov reached for the last lemon wedge set next to his glass of tea and sucked on it greedily. On rainy days like this his arm still ached from the old wound caused by the shrapnel blast in Beirut.

The pulpy fruit was sweet in comparison to the sour taste left in his mouth by the continuing success of Mack Bolan, the one-man army who had killed his only son, escaped the KGB's clutches, and even now waged war in every corner of the globe to thwart the ambitions of Moscow Center.

One of the phones on the table behind him buzzed softly. Strakhov swiveled and picked up the receiver. "What is it now, Maslovski?"

The latest aide, a man handpicked by Strakhov to replace the careless Vichinsky, cleared his throat with a nervous cough. He did not like to disturb the major general when he was taking his morning tea.

"It's Comrade Niktov, sir. He has called three times. Insists on speaking to you. I wasn't sure if..."

"Oh, put him through," Strakhov said wearily. What did the art expert want this time? Another favor from the KGB, a blind eye to his illicit dealings...in exchange for what? Only one thing interested Strakhov these days.

"My dear general," Niktov began flatteringly, "I have just received the most interesting tidbit of information from Paris."

So, thought Strakhov, this time the offer will come first and the favor will be requested later.

"The news will not appear in *Le Monde* until tomorrow's editions," continued the dealer, "and even then it might be overlooked."

"Well?"

"The Grand Duchess Marijana has passed away at last!" Niktov told him with a dry chuckle.

The head of the Thirteenth Section put down the half-chewed lemon wedge. His caller knew from the tense silence that he had Strakhov's undivided attention.

"I have learned there will be a very private funeral at the small church of Saint Bernard, the one near the Bois de Boulogne. It is set for two o'clock tomorrow afternoon."

"Thank you, Comrade Niktov. Your sense of social responsibility in reporting this matter will be remembered."

Strakhov cut the connection with one jab of his stubby finger and jiggled the phone to attract Maslovski, though no doubt his assistant was listening on an extension.

"Bring Gouzenkov to me."

It did not take long for Captain Maslovski to locate the Thirteenth Section's number-one hit man. Petr Gouzenkov, a Spetsnaz officer, had been a special advisor for a while in North Vietnam.

It was there that he had honed his lethal marksmanship. And it was also where he had acquired a taste for the perverse pleasures of recreational torture, which he practiced at every opportunity on captured American fliers. Or women and children if no POWs were at his disposal.

Now he liked to while away idle time in the interrogation rooms of the Lubyanka Prison, the grim jail immediately behind the KGB headquarters. That's where Maslovski found the butcher.

"Come in, come in," Strakhov invited with more than usual cordiality. The Kremlin's top killer could tell that the major general was excited.

The two men were a study of contrasts. Strakhov was heavy browed, his square face seamed with lines of experience gathered from the frigid days of Stalingrad through endless years of internal rivalries and struggles for power.

On the other hand, Gouzenkov was young, fit and sported a blond mane long enough to pass as fashionable in any cosmopolitan city, but his reptilian eyes were of such a pale gray-green tint that they seemed to stare right through whatever he fixed them on with unblinking steadiness.

Even Strakhov found it difficult to look the GRU captain straight in the face.

But for all their differences they shared two things in common: the blood of countless victims was on their hands, and they partook of a passionate hatred for the one target that eluded them both—Mack Bolan, once called Col. John Phoenix, also known as the Executioner.

"You have studied the American's file recently?"

"Right up-to-date, Major General." Gouzenkov nodded sharply.

"I know where he will be tomorrow afternoon. And he will be vulnerable." Strakhov announced his deduction in a conspiratorial whisper. "At a graveside in a Paris churchyard."

Gouzenkov's lips moved; it was not a smile, just a baring of his teeth.

"I want you to convey my greetings," ordered Strakhov. His fist slapped down hard on the desk. "In a 7.62 millimeter package."

Gouzenkov showed his enthusiasm for the first time. He knew it was every bit as much a personal vendetta for the older man as it was official KGB business. The Spetsnaz assassin nodded vigorously.

"I'll make sure the grave they are digging is for him."

Strakhov would not be satisfied until it was finished. "Do not fail me."

MACK BOLAN WAS PACKING the last of the needed items into a small case when the phone rang for a second time. It was probably the airline calling back to confirm his last-minute reservation.

"Hello?"

"Hi, Mack. This is Don. Don Edelman."

This time Bolan would not have recognized the caller's voice. It was tense, edgy, with a strained undercurrent of fear.

"Good to hear from you, Don." Bolan paused, momentarily puzzled. "But I must ask you how you got this number."

"I've still got a few contacts left in Washington, Mack. It took several calls I'll admit...a long talk with a Mr. Kurtzman...and an even longer explanation of who I was to Hal Brognola."

Bolan tested him one more time. "Where did we meet?"

"In Nam. The Steel Circle. I got the guided tour by a guy named Sergeant Mercy."

Uh-huh. It was Edelman. The ex-sniper would never forget the night patrol on which he had taken a green young journalist into the hellzone they called the Steel Circle.

In the blood-soaked hours of the jungle darkness they had won each other's respect. Edelman had learned the reality of that ugly conflict and why it was necessary and honorable for someone like Sgt. Mack Bolan to do the thankless tasks he did night after night.

For his part, the soldier found much to admire in a newsman who overcame his own fear to find out the facts for himself rather than make up another story in a hotel bar.

"I'm calling from Florida. I live down here now."

Bolan waited. He knew the writer was evading the issue, and that wasn't like him. Edelman had not called him just to reminisce. "What can I do for you, Don?"

"Keep me alive, maybe," came the curt reply.

Bolan needed more information.

"I think I've stumbled onto the biggest story of my career, if anyone will believe me. And it's one that would definitely interest you, that is, if half of what I've heard about you lately is true."

"Depends on who you've been listening to," replied Bolan evenly. "But about this story, give me some details."

"I can't, not on the phone." Edelman's hesitation showed he was even afraid to concede to whoever was eavesdropping that he knew his line was being tapped. "Could you come down here? Just for a couple of days. I promise you it won't be a wasted journey."

"When?"

"How about tonight?" The journalist's request was too urgent to be a joke.

"I'm sorry, Don, I have to go to Paris for a couple of days."

There was a brief pause at the other end before Edelman spoke again. "There's a direct flight back from London to Tampa. I could meet you at the airport."

"Okay. I'll see you the day after tomorrow. I'll be traveling as William Mercy."

"I'll be waiting for you."

EVEN THE PARIS SKIES seemed to mourn the passing of the Grand Duchess Marijana Rytova, as the sleek black hearse crunched along the gravel driveway that circled the neatly trimmed lots within the exclusive cemetery.

A thin drizzle, scarcely more than a mist, was drifting up from the Seine as the four men slid the coffin from its carrier.

Alexei Kirov was dressed in a navy blue overcoat. For years he had been Marijana's personal assistant, serving her as his family had always served the Rytova household. He signaled to the others that they should lift the wooden case to their shoulders.

It was a rather plain casket for such a grand old lady. But the duchess would be carried to her last resting place in the traditional style.

The tall American walked opposite Kirov. His brow was lightly beaded with perspiration. And it wasn't from the exertion of carrying so light a load.

Professor Stuart Farson, the controversial British historian, and young Igor Spasky, the great-grandson of the White Russian general who had fought so valiantly to stall the Bolsheviks when the allies retreated to Archangel during the intervention, were the two pallbearers who brought up the rear.

The only other mourner was Marijana's next-door neighbor, Monique Chabrol. Ten years before she had been the most sought-after fashion model in the world, but a drunken driver on the highway had put an end to her career, and almost her life. She was dragged from the wreckage of her Citroën still ablaze.

Since her recovery, Monique had hidden her disfigurement with veiled hats and sought refuge from the curious in the same quiet cul-de-sac that afforded privacy to the aging Russian aristocrat.

The duchess had been brought up in the Russian Orthodox faith. In France she had married a Roman Catholic writer, who was to be a martyr of the resistance, and in her later life she supported the evangelical work of the Gospel Light Mission, which smuggled Bibles and tracts into her beloved motherland.

The short memorial service had been fittingly ecumenical.

Now she was to be laid to rest next to her husband beneath the ancient elms of Saint Bernard.

But already the new Paris of steel and glass and concrete intruded on this quiet enclave, for the northern wall of the graveyard was overlooked by a giant apartment complex. Its myriad windows reflected the leaden clouds as the four men lowered the coffin.

The priest had finished his final blessing.

Kirov reached down and scattered a handful of the damp earth.

Bolan bent forward to do the same. Just as he moved to scoop up some dirt, he felt an explosive impact slam between his shoulder blades with excruciating force, pitching him headfirst into the open grave.

2

The priest's lips had been moving in silent prayer. Now his mouth hung open in slack-jawed surprise, shocked by this outrageous sacrilege.

Monique Chabrol screamed as the good-looking American lurched forward. Igor pulled her down behind the nearest headstone, a stone angel carrying a sword. Even in this moment of mortal peril the ex-model still clasped her hat in place to veil her scarred face.

Kirov had reached into his overcoat and pulled out a Luger. In one fluid movement he spun to face the apartment building. Sheer logic indicated that from the angle of the shot, that was the direction from which it must have been fired. But no sound had reached their ears. His eyes were angry slits in a gaunt face as he scanned the anonymous tower for any sign of the sniper.

Farson scrambled over the piled dirt and grabbed Bolan's body, pulling him back from the grave.

"Alexei. Here, give me a hand!"

Igor was escorting Monique toward the car at a fast trot. The priest had already scurried away.

Gun still in hand, the thin Russian pulled Bolan's arm over his shoulder. The two men, supporting the dead weight of the American's body between them, hurried down the slope. The Executioner's feet were dragging in the grass.

"HOW DO YOU FEEL?"

Bolan's shrug made him wince.

"His back is very badly bruised," the duchess's doctor explained to Kirov. He finished taping the dressing in place. "That should afford you some protection as long as you take it easy on yourself. The X rays show that no real damage was done to the spine. You are a very lucky man."

Bolan indicated the improved Kevlar-weave vest that he'd been wearing. "It was getting damn hot with that thing under my jacket."

"It could have been considerably hotter for you now if you had not been wearing it," Alexei reminded him with a wry smile. "I must admit your precautions were not in vain."

As soon as the medical officer had left them alone, Bolan asked, "Well, did you find anything?"

"No. The place was clean. No shell cases, no cigarette butts, no careless signs of his wait...nothing. We scoured every inch of the roof. This time Strakhov is using a real professional."

Neither man had any doubt as to who had dispatched the would-be assassin.

"So you have cheated him again, Mr. Bolan, perhaps even fooled him into thinking his plan has worked. You most certainly looked dead to the world when we dragged you to the car."

"I've bought some time, Alexei, maybe a few days. But he'll come after me." Bolan was not a man to delude himself. "I wouldn't report a confirmed hit in those circumstances."

"You, my friend, would have made certain." Kirov looked into those clear, cold eyes. "Even at that range you would have gone for the head shot."

THE PRESENCE OF BOTH Mack Bolan and Stuart Farson was requested at the reading of the Duchess Marijana's will.

In deference to the foreign visitors the lawyer had offered a summary in English, although they had managed to follow the gist of the first reading in French.

Alexei Kirov had been well looked after; his employer had left him more than ample funds to pursue his own campaign against the Soviet usurpers, the battle they had shared through all their years together.

A special bequest was made to a veterinarian's home for stray cats and a great deal of money was to be given in support of the Gospel Light's efforts to spread the Good Word to the enslaved people of Eastern Europe.

The English professor was given a generous gift for his service in exposing the nefarious workings of the Kremlin's subversive units. The duchess had noted that she hoped Professor Farson would be encouraged to continue his work.

And a very considerable portion of her immense fortune had been left in trust to underwrite Mack Bolan's ongoing war against their mutual enemy: the KGB and its worldwide network of terrormongers.

THE AIR WAS HEAVY with a thick haze of blue smoke. Professor Farson had convened this secret meeting—part seminar, part informal briefing, part intelligence exchange—in the two-hour wait they had for the return flight to Heathrow.

Sitting across from Bolan were Jacques Terrence, a Sûreté expert on the narcotics trade, and Stefan Metz, an Interpol undercover agent who had penetrated more drug rings from Turkey to Thailand than any other man still alive to talk about it.

"Mack, you told me you wanted the very latest intelligence on the drug trade," said the Englishman, acting as the small group's unofficial chairman. "Well, these are the men who can fill you in. Monsieur Terrence here cleaned up the Marseilles end of the French Connection."

"You know what happened to the heroin that was seized in that bust?" asked the unhappy French official.

"It vanished," said Bolan.

"Yes, it was replaced by flour in the very police lockers where it was supposed to be protected as evidence," said Terrence. "That is history now, but it underlines the single biggest problem we have in dealing effectively with the drug smugglers."

"Corruption," continued Metz, emphasizing the word with a gesture of contempt. "Bribery taints every organized effort to stop the contraband. The amounts of money involved are so huge nowadays that they can pay off whoever they please—right to the very top."

"Smuggling into the United States via the Caribbean pipeline has reached epidemic proportions," noted Farson glumly. "I'm not sure what one man working alone can do to help stop the flow."

Bolan recounted some of his recent exploits against the crime families in New York. The three men were impressed by what he had accomplished but shared his frustration in knowing that these hit-and-run strikes were stopgap victories at best.

"You are going up against more than a handful of underworld figures now, Mr. Bolan," warned the Sûreté man. "An alliance of evil is being forged between the newly rich Colombian clans, the old Mafia families and certain unfriendly governments."

"Cuba is taking over as the center of operations for running drugs into America," continued Metz. "And Castro himself is the mastermind."

"I thought one of the first orders of business for Castro's revolution was to clear the gangsters out of Havana." Bolan's remark was unmistakably ironic. "Why the hell would he want to dirty his hands with drug smuggling?"

"Once again, Mr. Bolan, the answer is money."

"As you well know, Mack, from the very beginning Cuba has been a vassal state to the Soviet Union. Right now, by conservative estimates, it's costing the Kremlin more than ten million dollars a day to keep the island afloat," Farson told them as he relit his pipe. "Castro has an ego as big as his beard. Being a Russian puppet does not sit well with him. He has adventurous ambitions of his own. The trouble is that when the KGB says jump, he can only ask, How high? And even the secret police, the Cuban Dirección General de Inteligencia that keeps him in power, is merely a branch-office operation of Moscow Center."

"And if he regains some of his independence, a little breathing space, he will need his own police network, one that is loyal only to him," said Bolan, filling in the colors for himself.

"Precisely. And that costs money," Metz added, borrowing one of his colleague's Gitanes and lighting up. "That's why he's gone into the drug business. What better way to fund his own dreams of glory and, at the same time, help undermine his bitterest foe, the United States?"

"He makes the so-called French Connection look like—how do you say?—nickel-and-dime stuff," said Jacques Terrence. "Every night boats leave ports in Cuba loaded with cocaine and bales of Colombian pot for deliveries in the gulf coast of Texas to the Carolinas and beyond."

"The principal runs, of course, are over the shortest routes to Florida," said Metz. "A single vessel might be carrying, say, a hundred kilos of coke. That's worth at least twenty-five million dollars on the street. You can imagine what Castro is grossing per year just from his cut of the action."

"What about these new antismuggling forces that were established by the President?" asked Bolan.

"They have been effective to a point," said Terrence. "As an observer I was attached to the Federal South Florida Task Force last year. But there are so many agencies involved that everyone is tripping over someone else's feet. Besides, they are as publicity hungry as any other bureaucrats and make a media mountain out of every molehill bust. They are not empowered to tackle the problem at its source. After all, a raid into Cuba could very easily touch off a global war!"

"I hate to repeat myself," added Metz, who had developed informants in the most unlikely places, "but almost every man has his price. These new agencies report endless attempts at bribery. Sometimes it must have worked.''

''But with all the cutters, radar, spotter blimps and stoolies they have working for them, they cannot stop the shipments from getting through. It is as if the drug runners know exactly where the task force will strike next.'' Despite his first-hand experience, Terrence was clearly puzzled.

''I'm on my way to Florida tomorrow,'' said Bolan. ''I've got some personal business to attend to, but I'll look into this.''

''If you can find out how the smugglers succeed in off-loading their cargoes across the most closely guarded straits in the world, then you'll have accomplished more than all the antidrug squads put together.'' The French-man looked skeptical. ''I wish you luck, Mr. Bolan.''

''I can give you one name to go on,'' said Stefan Metz. ''Maria Ortega, if that's what she still calls herself.''

Terrence was surprised. ''You mean the girl who was once Castro's mistress?''

''Yes. And before that she was known to consort with Capt. Carlos Porcallo.''

''A founding member of the DGI,'' filled in Farson. ''Sometimes called *el loco*—the crazy one. He's a mean-tempered bastard.''

''Reliable sources tell me that Porcallo is now running Castro's smuggling business on a day-to-day level.''

''Where is this Maria Ortega?'' asked Bolan.

''Castro got tired of her. He dumped her with a lot of other people he wanted to get rid of out of Mariel Harbor.''

''You mean she was a refugee?''

''She's living somewhere in Florida now,'' said Metz.

''Let's continue this in the car,'' said Farson, checking his watch. ''We've got to get to the airport.''

3

The beige Chrysler was no longer there. It was the third time Edelman had checked in an hour. From behind the net curtains he scanned the gravel road that led down to the waterfront house. Edelman focused the binoculars on the clump of greenery that marked the driveway of his nearest neighbors, the Balcombs.

They were a Canadian couple who came down to enjoy the Florida sunshine from December to March each year. Sometimes they lent their pink stucco bungalow to friends; but they usually dropped Edelman a postcard to tell him about such an arrangement.

The big gum-chewing guy in the Panama who had parked his Chrysler half-concealed behind the Balcombs' gate had not appeared to be a friend of the family. From the glimpse Edelman got of the patient watcher, it was hard to imagine him as being anyone's friend.

Now the car was gone. It had vanished as silently as it had appeared that morning. Must be getting paranoid, the writer told himself, but he took one last long look through the binoculars just to make sure.

The front section of his house was built on stilts so that it was propped over the water. It was this veranda with its uninterrupted view of every glorious sunset that had sold Don Edelman on the place six years ago. His office, converted from one of the front bedrooms, had a studio window that looked out across the water to the low hummocks that dotted the bay beyond Pelican Key.

He returned to his desk and tried to concentrate. The work area to the side of his typewriter was littered with photographs of ships and salvage men, nautical tables, cruising guides to the intricate coves and cays of the Florida coast, reels of recording tape and first-draft notes on yellow newsprint.

Edelman shifted the tarnished doubloon that weighed down the corner of a big chart, zigzagged the parallel rules up from the compass rose and reexamined the alternate courses he had already penciled in.

His finger rested on the marking *Betsy Lou* for a moment, and then he added a question mark after this inscription. Very carefully he drew in yet another shaded square alongside the name.

Edelman tapped the pencil nervously against the edge of the draftman's table he used for his chart work. He reached over to the corkboard above the phone and ripped off the memo. "Mercy. Pan Am from London. Arr. 4:00 P.M." Then he stuffed the note into his pocket.

He checked the time. It was just after one o'clock. The airport was a good two-hour drive from Pelican Key. And although he knew that flight was often late, Edelman wanted to be there when the plane landed.

There was a mismatched mound of radio and recording equipment heaped against the far wall of the office, a jumble of wires, receivers, filters and tape decks. Edelman flipped on a switch and a familiar voice flooded the room with hell-fire oratory.

"And I say again, we must be ready to stand up and be counted. We must be ready to resist the heathen Russian hordes.

"This is not a do-nothing ministry and I know that you—yes, every one of you listening out there—aren't the kind to bury your heads in the sand of liberal complacency. I want you to go right now—yes, right this minute!—and find a postcard, a note pad, even a scrap of paper will do, and write to your congressman and write to your senator and tell them you support the defense program, and the antidrug program, and the immigration control program...because we must keep this land of ours safe and secure, pure and undefiled.

"We must be ready, my friends. We must be ready to keep our appointment with the Lord...."

Edelman opened a fresh bottle of Scotch and poured himself a stiff shot as the organ music swelled to a crescendo behind the urgent voice of Magnus Angell.

"Turn with me now to the refuge, the rock, the Good Book. And, my friends, if you don't already have your own gilt-edged copy of the *Appointment with the Lord* Bible, just send in $9.95 to this station, KRST, and my volunteers will mail one to you. So now, let us examine Isaiah 26, verse 21, and I quote, 'For, behold, the Lord cometh out of his place to punish the inhabitants of the earth for their iniquity...'

"What a message! We should heed these words...."

Edelman jotted down the chapter and verse numbers, turned on the recorder, shut off the speakers and watched the level meters. He did not want to miss any of today's broadcast.

It was time to leave.

Edelman gulped down the last of the whiskey. He held out his hands straight in front of him for a moment. He really did not want Mack Bolan to see how badly he'd gotten the shakes.

BOLAN HAD SPENT THE NIGHT at Stuart Farson's house on the southern downs of England. The two men had sat until late into the night talking, mulling over every detail supplied by Jacques Terrence and Stefan Metz.

The bottom line had come down to this: how did the drug smugglers safely evade all the coast-watching precautions arrayed against them? How did they know when and where to off-load their deadly cargoes?

They still had nothing but guesswork and question marks when the American finally climbed the stairs to the cozy guest room. Bolan's back ached from the massive bruise. It took him a long time to feel drowsy and then, just as he was dozing off at last, the phone rang.

"That was Jacques Terrence," explained Farson, standing wrapped in a heavy woolen dressing gown. "I took the liberty of asking him to put out feelers for any known 'unfriendlies' who might have been at work in Paris."

"Who did he come up with?"

"A man named Petr Gouzenkov."

Bolan shook his head. The name didn't mean anything.

"A top gun for the KGB. Captain Gouzenkov is a GRU-Spetsnaz specialist seconded to work with the Thirteenth Section," said the professor. "Personally groomed by Greb Strakhov and held in reserve for special missions only. I've got some notes and photos of him in my files. Anyway, he arrived at Orly at ten o'clock yesterday morning, traveling as a cultural envoy to the Soviet embassy.''

"Sounds like the usual cover."

"Jacques also told me that another Russian, supposedly a correspondent for TASS, has been asking a lot of questions about the funeral," Farson went on, "and I was thinking that priest might have talked."

"Sooner or later, they'll find out." Bolan was not going to lose any more sleep over it. He had to be up early to return to Heathrow for the Tampa flight....

"Can I get you a pillow, sir?" The stewardess's voice broke into Bolan's thoughts.

"Yes, please."

A few moments later, the flight attendant returned with the pillow and Bolan stuffed it down behind his back. It was going to feel like a long flight.

His thoughts raced ahead to Florida.

How much time was he prepared to spend tracing Maria Ortega? Among the increasing numbers of Cuban exiles who crowded into southern Florida, it would be like looking for the proverbial needle in a haystack. What could she tell him about Porcallo's work in first setting up the Castro pipeline? And anyway, would she be willing to talk?

First he had to find out what had got Don Edelman so rattled—the guy sounded truly in fear for his life.

Bolan himself had lived with that ever-present threat for so long that it was second nature to him now. That's the way it was on the front line, any front line.

Edelman had been plenty scared the night Bolan had escorted him inside the Steel Circle, but he'd coped with that fear, just as he'd coped with having all his journalistic preconceptions overturned.

After the diplomats had sold out at a faraway conference table, abandoning their allies to a gruesome fate and leaving hundreds of good men listed MIA, Edelman had sat down and written the first realistic novel about the final phases of the war. The book was a thinly fictionalized account of a line sniper's missions deep behind enemy lines.

The public had not been ready for a story that spelled out the way it really was—they still preferred to believe in the glib television version—and, in knee-jerk unison, the liberal critics hated it. Don persevered with an analysis of failed strategy in Southeast Asia. Again the public did not want to be reminded of what was easier to forget.

After that the embittered young writer went to Europe.

He made some friends around Marseilles, visited the headquarters of the Foreign Legion at Aubagne and started writing a series of legionnaire stories that became highly successful.

They did not make him a millionaire, but they brought him back to the States and paid for his private retreat, the unusual waterfront property on Pelican Key.

Bolan had picked up a copy of the latest Foreign Legion adventure at Heathrow. *Escape from Hell* told the little-known story of the handful of legionnaires who had managed to break through the Vietminh stranglehold on Dien Bien Phu.

He flipped it open and read the dedication. "To the man who opened my eyes—Sergeant Mercy."

THE BIG JET was twenty minutes late landing in Tampa.

At Passport Control Bolan was asked to step to one side. A tall man wearing shiny boots and an even shinier holster, ushered him into one of the immigration offices.

"Mr. Mercy, my name is Creswell. I'm from the sheriff's office." His tone was conciliatory. "We just had a call from our colleagues in Big Pine County."

Bolan was still not sure quite what to expect. His expression gave away nothing.

"There's been an accident. I'm afraid Mr. Don Edelman was killed in a mishap there this afternoon. They've just pulled his car out of the canal. The deputy in charge found a note of some kind in his pocket, apparently a memo about your arrival time here in Tampa."

"Thank you for acting so promptly."

"I'm sorry to be the one to bring you the bad news," said Creswell.

So Don Edelman had a right to be scared, but it didn't alter the fact that Bolan had arrived too late.

Too late to save his friend's life, but not too late to find the killer.

4

"I expect Sheriff Johnson will want to talk to you," Creswell had told him at the airport.

But Bolan knew Sheriff Buford Johnson could not have cared less for anything that the visitor might have told him. The lawman's mind was already made up about the accident.

"Careless sonofabitch. Why does the county pay to put up road signs? Hell, he must have passed it enough times!" With one sweep of his hamlike paw, Johnson indicated the yellow markers at either side of the bridge. Bolan had already seen the one on the way in; it read Slippery When Wet.

Johnson's deputy, an acne-pitted youth with straw-colored hair, was still measuring the skid marks.

It seemed to Bolan that the whole thing was pretty well cut and dried as far as the police were concerned. They had been in no hurry to investigate the scene, but Bolan's arrival seemed to rattle the sheriff. "Hey, Gilman, you taken the pictures yet?" Johnson shouted.

Gilman wound up the measuring tape, then sauntered over to the sheriff's car to pick up the camera.

It appeared that Don Edelman had approached the bridge—a plain span floored with metal grating—swerved at the last moment, skidded sideways onto the

treacherous surface, smashed through the wooden
guardrail and plunged down into the brown water of
Marriot's Swamp.

The car was waiting at the far end of the bridge, still
hooked up to the red tow truck that had pulled it up the
bank. Don's body had been taken to the morgue.

"Looks like the right front tire shredded on this grating," said Johnson.

"Yeah. Or maybe he—"

"Swerved because of a blowout." Johnson cut off
Bolan's observation. He didn't need a stranger teaching
him his job. "Probably a coon or, uh, a deer ran out in
front of him. I heard tell Edelman had a soft spot for
animals. Then again I also heard he'd had his trouble
with booze."

Bolan shrugged. He honestly didn't know what Don's
drinking habits were these days.

"Well, the coroner's report will fill in the details."
Johnson hitched up his trousers, but his beer-gut stub-
bornly drooped over his belt. "You staying nearby, mister? We contacted his agent, some guy in Miami, and he's
going to look after the necessary arrangements."

Bolan picked up the signal loud and clear. He wasn't
welcome in Big Pine County.

"Uh uh. There's no reason for me to stay."

Johnson walked away with a satisfied nod.

Bolan looked at the car. The right front end was badly
crumpled from its impact with the wooden railing.

"Say, mister, you're in the way," complained Gilman.

"Sorry." Bolan stepped to one side so the deputy could
take the final photograph. Then Gilman signaled that the
tow-truck driver could proceed back to town. "Tell me,
what time did it rain today?"

"Let's see, I was coming back from a coffee break...oh, maybe about three-fifteen. Out here it would have passed through, say, twenty minutes or half an hour earlier than in town."

"Thanks." Bolan walked to the splintered railing and lit a cigarette. The bank was gouged with the tracks of Don's car being dragged out of the swamp water.

Johnson hooted impatiently. Deputy Gilman obediently trotted back to the car. The sheriff executed a three-point turn and spewed grit as he accelerated toward town.

Bolan watched them go. Even the sheriff's car sported a bumper sticker that read, Are You Ready for Your Appointment with the Lord? Bolan smoked a second cigarette, waiting to ensure that Johnson was not coming back to give him his marching orders again.

The car he had rented at the airport was parked on the shoulder a safe distance from the bridge. He now stood there alone.

The faded greenery of Marriot's Swamp stretched away in all directions, rustling, croaking and slithering with unseen wildlife. The brackish water glided silkily around the pilings.

Bolan had risked a very expensive speeding ticket to get here and the drive had taken him just over an hour. He figured that by traveling at a more leisurely pace to meet the London plane, Don would have had to allow two hours or more to reach Tampa. And the writer would have passed over this bridge at least a full hour before the rains fell.

He paced slowly along both sides of the road, parallel to the skid marks. Although the tow truck and Johnson's vehicle had chewed up the shoulders in places, there were no signs of animal tracks in the mud on either embankment.

Bolan walked back across the bridge.

On each side of the turbid waterway was a solid phalanx of semitropical vegetation, but it did not take a man with Bolan's experience too long to find a narrow path threading through the buttonwoods. It never strayed too far from the edge of the canal.

About four hundred yards from the road there was a large fallen tree trunk. Bolan found what he was looking for on the other side of this moss-covered log. The rotting remains of a wooden jetty stood at the mouth of a small cut draining into the main channel.

He turned, leaning experimentally against the spongy bark, and found he had a clear view of the west end of the bridge. The side Don Edelman had approached from. The broken guardrail hung over the side at a drunken angle.

The damp ground had been trampled by someone who had waited for quite a while at this precise spot. And whoever it was, they chewed gum. Bolan picked up two chewing-gum wrappers from the mud.

Farther up the cut he could see the ground had been scored by the keel of a shallow draft skiff. It had been pulled out of sight up into the bushes. The straight track of the boat's underside was filled with rainwater.

Bolan went back to the fallen tree. He quartered the ground, searching each square thoroughly. He came across some rusted hooks and a tangle of ten-pound test, probably cast aside by a frustrated fisherman who had used the small pier. Bolan took his time and it paid off. Nestled among an interwoven clump of mangrove roots was a cartridge case.

Carefully he extracted the evidence: a 7.62mm NATO heavy round. Bolan weighed the casing in the palm of his hand. He guessed that Edelman's front tire was blown out by a M1A Super Match. Using an ART IV scope to sight with, it would not have been a difficult shot.

Bolan retraced his steps through the bushes back to his car. The drug smugglers would have to wait. He wanted to find out what information his friend had that would get him killed.

It was less than six miles to the far point of Pelican Key.

A few sand-blown mobile homes were clustered around a small general store that had long since closed. A rusted Coca Cola sign creaked in the early-evening breeze. And the paving gave way to a graveled track.

Bolan frowned as he took in the hardy scrub and salt grass encroaching on the dirt road. Don Edelman had sure picked an out-of-the-way spot to do his writing.

The Executioner passed a pink bungalow that appeared deserted, then the road ran down to a dead end outside Don's place.

It took Bolan two minutes to pick the lock and let himself in. The entrance led into the kitchen and the main rooms were at the front of the house overlooking the ocean.

A bottle of Scotch stood on the Formica countertop. Bolan checked the contents. It looked as if a double or less had been poured from it. He stepped over and peered into the garbage canister by the sink—no empties in there. So that blew a hole in the sheriff's other snide remark.

Bolan wanted to check out the office. He crossed the hallway and tried the first door.

Well-honed combat senses told him that someone was in there, waiting.

But this time even that split-second intuition was not enough warning.

5

The door slammed into his face, pinning him against the jamb. Then a huge man wearing a Panama jumped out and fired a right cross to Bolan's head.

The Executioner jerked his head back, but still the attacker's fist caught him a glancing blow along his temple.

Bolan crashed back in the corridor. But even as he fell he hooked one foot behind the other man's ankle, while the sole of his right shoe hacked into the intruder's skin. The man went down hard.

He grunted in annoyance as he was dumped on the floor. The straw hat flew off, beneath it he was as bald as a billiard ball.

They were both back on their feet together.

The big goon came through the doorway with a speed surprising for a man of his bulk. Head tucked down, he drove hard into Bolan's midriff.

Two hundred sixty-five pounds of what seemed like solid bone smashed the Executioner back into the wall. The whole house shook on its stilts with the fury of the assault. Bolan winced as daggers of pain shot through his spine. This was not what the French doctor had meant by "take it easy on yourself." In one rasping rush the wind was knocked out of him.

Working on reflex, Bolan chopped inward with ax-edged hands, but to little effect. Baldy didn't have a neck to speak of. He gave an exasperated snort, shook his bullet head to clear it, took the measure of Bolan's feint and then with one massive shove sent him sprawling down the length of the hallway.

Bolan slithered to a sickeningly sudden stop as the back of his skull cracked against the antique cannonball Don had used as a doorstop. Through a red-misted haze he saw the steely flash of a switchblade appear in his enemy's hand.

With a reptilian grimace, the bald man was calmly preparing to carve him up.

Suddenly there was a crunch of gravel as a car pulled up outside.

The knifeman made a quick calculation. He didn't have time to reach Bolan and slice him. Instead he fled back into the office as abruptly as he came in.

Bolan struggled to his elbow. The full-length glass windows in Don's study were being dragged open. Bolan climbed to his feet.

Above the ringing in his ears, he heard a powerful outboard cough to life. He tried to move quickly toward the windows leading out onto the deck. But the long aluminum skiff had pulled well clear. The bald man glanced back once, opened the throttle wide and surged around the headland.

"What the hell's going on here?" asked the smartly dressed newcomer. "Who are you?"

"I'm a friend of Don's," Bolan replied. He pointed to the wake left by the speeding boat. "But I don't think he was."

"Well, what happened?" the other man demanded impatiently.

"I came down to the house after I'd stopped at the scene of the, er, accident, I think Johnson's calling it," Bolan said. "And that big ape was already here. He jumped me."

"A thief? A burglar taking advantage..."

There was no sign that the room had been rifled.

"He didn't hit like a burglar." Bolan did not feel like explaining why his back was on fire.

The man hesitated for a moment, unsure what to do next. He put down his briefcase. "You're Mack Bolan, aren't you? The guy Don met in Vietnam, the one in that picture?"

They both glanced at the eight-by-ten color print hanging on the study wall.

Bolan remembered that it had been taken by a bar girl in Saigon a couple of weeks after their foray into the Steel Circle. No wonder the stranger was wavering. A plastic surgery session so many lifetimes ago had altered Bolan's features.

"Yeah, that was me. I guess I've changed." Bolan did not feel like explaining that, either. Besides, he had some questions of his own. "Who are you? Don's agent?"

"Yes. Let me introduce myself. I'm Peter Ziman. I left Miami the moment I heard the terrible news. Drove straight across. I still can't believe what happened."

"Believe it. It happens to us all sooner or later. Don just got unlucky, I guess."

The thin businessman bent forward, retrieved the Panama and stood there awkwardly.

"It belonged to Baldy," Bolan said, taking it from the agent's hand and checking around the inner band for a label. The Head Shoppe, Tampa.

Ziman rearranged the silk handkerchief in his breast pocket and brushed an imaginary speck of dirt from the front of his linen suit. He stared at the papers stacked next to Don's typewriter and wondered aloud, "Maybe he completed enough of the first draft to have it finished by a ghost."

It was a ghoulish expression to use under the circumstances, but Bolan understood what he had in mind. It also gave him a clearer picture of the agent's sense of priorities. "Tell me, what kind of book was Don writing this time?"

"*Treasures of the Deep* is the working title. We're expecting good things from it," Ziman told him, beginning to leaf through the copy. "Don had a lot of success with his Foreign Legion series, but he still liked to keep his hand in popular nonfiction. This one is an up-to-the-minute report on the treasure hunters working off the Florida coast."

Bolan's interest was aroused. A book on treasure divers. That took care of why the office was littered with charts and other nautical paraphernalia. But it still did not clarify why Don had thought it would be of such personal interest to the Executioner. And he still couldn't tell why Don had brought him all the way down to Florida. Whatever it was had got him killed.

Ziman was still glancing through the sheets of yellow rough, engrossed in Don's story. Bolan was curious how all the radio and taping equipment tied in with the book Edelman was writing. The Executioner rewound the cassette already in the machine, stopping it halfway, then pushed the Play button.

"And that's why we must be ready! The Lord never said it would be easy. We have to keep a constant vigil…''

Ziman's head jerked up; he was startled by the voice coming out of the tape recorder.

"Magnus Angell! Why on earth would Don be taping that windbag?''

Bolan wondered the same thing. "Who is he?''

"Angell? Anti-Castro, anti-Red, antiabortion, anti-drugs, antidrinking…just about anti-everything. And he's becoming the most popular preacher in the South. He's building some kind of health and media complex up at Alachalafaya. Radio, television station—the works.''

Ziman resumed his reading but Bolan let the tape play for a minute.

"The message is loud and clear. Look at Jeremiah 23, verse 10. Doesn't that tell you something, my friends? Yes, it's all written down in black and white. Listen to God's word…''

Ziman looked up again. This time he gave a cynical shrug. "How a guy who preaches against almost anything that's fun can bring in so many donations is beyond me.''

Perhaps Magnus Angell's listeners did not share the same sense of fun as the suave Floridian, thought Bolan, but he didn't say anything. He moved across to the chart table. Don's cryptic markings did not make a great deal of sense at first glance, but they seemed to indicate a search pattern.

"I think it might be one of the current salvage dives Don was following for the book,'' Ziman commented.

"Could be." Despite his own fatalistic remark, Bolan found himself annoyed at how easily the agent referred to Don in the past tense. "Except *Betsy Lou* doesn't sound like the name of a Spanish galleon."

Ziman ignored the remark as he scooped the papers together and slid them into his briefcase.

"I'd like to borrow this chart for a couple of days. I want to find out what Don was up to. You can have it back as soon as you need it."

Peter Ziman frowned at the request, but then reluctantly nodded his assent.

"And a couple of other things. I'd like to borrow Don's camera and this portable tape recorder."

Bolan sensed that the agent was about to draw the line. It was time to spell it out for him.

"Look, I'm not convinced that Don's death was quite the accident it appeared to be. I've got some questions. I just want to ask around, that's all. Would you type up a short note over your signature as an agent, introducing me as a journalist doing some research. Call me Mark Bailey. It'll save a lot of explanations."

Ziman slowly rolled a sheet of paper into the typewriter. While he was concentrating on pecking out an open introduction, Bolan slipped a couple of the cassettes into his pocket. He also pocketed a photo of Don and a sailor—maybe a fishing buddy—drinking beer in the cockpit of a trawler.

"Here, will this do?"

Bolan skimmed the note. "Yeah, thanks."

Bolan drove back toward Tampa, but stopped short of the city to register at the Palm Court Motel.

He stood soaking in the shower, letting the warm jets massage his back. But his thoughts would not be so easily soothed. Where was Gouzenkov now? How long would it take Strakhov's marksman to find out his intended victim had escaped once more? And who was the bald gorilla sneaking around Don's place?

Mack Bolan did not like being forced on the defensive. He was uncomfortable when operating from a reaction-only mode. Those days on the run from Zubrovna after the Macek assassination still burned fresh in his memory. It was the same way he'd felt in Japan when he was trapped between the *yakuza* and the treacherous Kingoro Nakada. But most of all he remembered those kill-crazy days after the Palm Springs wipeout when the Executioner's Mafia campaign was just beginning.

This was still a guerrilla war. The terrain varied, the rules remained the same. He had to seize the initiative. Whether in the tangled undergrowth of Southeast Asia or in the concrete wilderness of the urban jungles back home, it was the aggressor who held the aces.

It was a lesson first learned in Nam.

A white-hot truth that was peril to ignore.

It was time for Bolan to switch to attack mode. But first he had to identify the enemy. Then locate them.

And it had to be done fast—before the savages knew what was about to hit them.

To complete these first two essential steps as quickly as they had to be done, Bolan needed someone he could depend on.

Bolan spent a precious moment thinking of Antonio Esparza, Toro, a courageous warrior whom the Executioner had befriended and whose help he had enlisted in his first Miami blitz. And again when Bolan had learned of a Cuban exile tie-in with the Mafia crime machine. He broke Toro out of jail the second time.

At the end of the mission, Toro was not so lucky.

Luck, right.

Something that appeared to be in short supply these days, especially for those brave soldiers who took up the Executioner's cause.

The names were written in blood, their own, for all the world to see, but Bolan couldn't help thinking that those names were invisible to all but himself.

A grim reminder, sure.

Of his mortality.

Of the need to keep his battle senses wary and never falter.

Or pay the supreme price.

This was no time for ghosts, but for the living, damn straight. Bolan shrugged it off, concentrating on the present.

He needed help to engage the savages once more. And he had an idea where to find it.

Bolan left the motel and drove to the nearest public phone booth. He placed a call to Johnny Bolan at Strongbase in San Diego.

"It's me, John."

No hesitation on the other end as the younger Bolan made the connection.

"Always good to hear from you, Sentinel. How's the heat in Florida? I listened to your itinerary on the tape and I figured you'd be there by now. Too bad about the duchess."

"A great lady. But she was getting on." Bolan looked at his watch. The numbers were falling rapidly. "Look, John, I'll fill you in when I get back. But right now I need a favor."

"Shoot."

And the thought didn't escape Bolan that he'd be doing a lot of it soon. Very soon.

"Get in touch with Virginia immediately. Ask her for Mr. Art Intel. I need a family backgrounder on Pescado. I'll wait for your call at this number." Bolan read off the phone booth's number, hung up, then walked back to his car to wait for the information.

The Executioner fired a cigarette as he leaned on the front fender of his rented wheels. He figured that if there was a tap on Strongbase in San Diego, his coded message would buy him some time.

Bolan was glad that he had used spare moments when he was not in the field to devise a list of code words with Johnny for just such emergencies. Virginia, of course, was the location of Stony Man Farm; Art Intel was short for artificial intelligence, a term popularly used to refer to the computer field; and Aaron Kurtzman was the resident computer expert at Stony Man. Pescado was the nickname given to Rafael Encizo because of his underwater expertise.

The shrill jangle of the public telephone intruded on Bolan's thoughts. He flicked the butt to the pavement and snared the receiver.

"Go ahead, John."

"The info Virginia gave me is quite extensive. Could you narrow it down to specifics?"

"Yeah. Does Pescado have any relatives in Miami? I can vaguely recall something like this when I lived with Virginia."

"Correct. There is a cousin. Son of Pescado's mother's sister. The name is Pedro Estrada. He's a private investigator, a good one. Works mainly in the Hispanic community. Back in Cuba he worked in some kind of underground organization against the Castro government. He was known by close friends as *el espectro*. That's Spanish for the ghost. I've got a phone number and an address.''

Bolan memorized the data, thumbed a coin into the slot and dialed the number that Johnny gave him.

There were a few clicks and hums, then a recorded message came on. "This is Pedro Estrada. At the tone leave your name and number and I'll get back to you.''

Bolan waited until the high-pitched beep ended before he spoke.

"I'm a friend of your cousin, Rafael. He may have talked to you in the past. My name is Phoenix. I need your help. I'm staying at the Palm Court Motel. If you've heard of me, you'll find me.''

6

It can cloak a man. Or it can kill him. The night makes no friends.

He could feel an unaccustomed pressure tugging at his back. It was Edelman, his hand clamped tight to Bolan's knapsack.

Branches reached out to scratch at them. Roots tried to snare them. Damp leaves, like fingers wet with blood, brushed his forehead. They moved forward through the Stygian darkness.

Somewhere before them a booby-trap trip wire was stretched out across the path. And Charlie was right on their tail. They were running a gauntlet of sudden death in the middle of a maze called the Steel Circle, in the blood-soaked center of a jungle hellzone.

It was just another night in Vietnam.

Bolan sensed the VC patrol was gaining on them fast. He pushed Edelman to one side into the tall grass. The writer must have been screaming inside to know what was happening. But he controlled his rookie fears. And that took courage. Bolan had rolled off the path in the other direction.

The track exploded in a jittering confusion of flying earth and shredded twigs as the VC opened fire.

Three muzzle-flashes.

Bolan swung the M-16 and squeezed off.

Full auto!

White-hot flame seared the pitch-black undergrowth as the weapon spat out a staccato crescendo of destruction.

Screams. Thrashing. Writhing. Blind stumbling. A bellowed threat.

Bolan slammed in a fresh magazine and let the rifle reply.

Rat-tat-tat...

He was awake at the first sharp tap, rolled off the bed and checked through the window before opening the door.

They eyed each other for a moment, and from what he saw, Bolan knew instinctively that he could trust this man. Behind the casually expensive clothes Bolan sensed a true warrior.

The corners of his eyes were lined; silver threaded the dark hair above his ears. But it was the white flash of his smile that convinced Bolan.

"Mr. Phoenix. I am Pedro Estrada. I have met with my cousin, Rafael, a few times over the past few years. He told me of the work you do, *señor*. He spoke of you with great respect. This is why I answered your message."

Bolan thrust out his hand and invited Estrada into the motel room.

"Would you like a drink?" Bolan asked.

"*Gracias*, no. Too early for me."

Bolan eyed the man with new respect.

"How can I help you, Mr. Phoenix?"

"Please, call me Mack. In my business a man has to wear many faces. I left my Phoenix face behind some time ago. Tell me, why do they call you *espectro*?"

Estrada lit a dark Cuban cigarette and watched the first thick plume of smoke billow toward the ceiling before he began to speak.

"Like you, *señor*, a man has to hide his identity, sometimes even himself. I fought for the cause of a free Cuba. It was not easy. I organized raids against the authorities. Huge rewards were put on my head. But they never could find me.

"I will not pretend that all my countrymen are saints— a few became turncoats, informers, while others joined the Mob. It was then I knew I had to leave, but try to continue the fight from some other place. I could have gone to South America, but I wanted to be close to my Cuba.

"Then, in 1980, came Mariel Harbor. Castro thought it was an easy way to get rid of his problems, but in all that confusion we managed to get several men ashore. And so, *amigo*, the fight against *el culebra* is more active than ever."

Estrada took another deep drag. Bolan noticed that when he spoke of Cuba and the cause of freedom his accent became thicker, reverting to the softness and sibilance of his mother tongue.

There was a glitter in the depths of those serious brown eyes.

"It may be years before I can set foot once more in my homeland. I will never give up the fight. Never! But for now I will help you, *señor*. You have only to ask."

"I need two things, my friend: information and supplies."

"I can guess the kind of supplies you're after. What sort of information?"

"I'm trying to locate two people—for quite different reasons. One is a man who jumped me shortly after my arrival here. Big, bullet headed and bald. Wears a Panama. Shops in Tampa. And just might be an habitual gum chewer."

"Does he carry a knife?"

"Biggest damn switchblade I ever saw."

"Sounds like Bull Oakum."

"Who does he work for?"

"Anyone who has *dinero*. He is too, how do you say, crazy, to be on any regular payroll. He hires himself out to different gangs along the gulf. I have not seen him for a while. I can ask around, find out where he is."

"I'll be grateful," Bolan said. "And perhaps one day I can be of help to you."

"Perhaps. Who else do you want to find out about?"

"Maria Ortega. At least, that was her name in Cuba."

Estrada shrugged. It did not ring any bells with him.

"An artist, painter, something like that. She used to run with Castro's inner circle, maybe even bedded down with Fidel himself. Anyway, in 1980 she got the push."

"From Mariel Harbor to Florida?"

"Right. She landed here that May. I've got nothing on her since."

"Where was she from originally?"

"I'm not sure. She first attracted notice as the girl-friend of Capt. Carlos Porcallo."

"*El loco!* Many people would like to get their hands on him." Estrada's eyes gave away the fact that he would be the first in line. "Probably means she's from northern Camagüey. Okay, *amigo*, I'll see what I can find out."

"Now, about those supplies…"

"Modern, dependable firepower?"

Bolan nodded. Estrada understood perfectly.

"Wait here. I have some 'samples' that I was going to send to friends back home."

It was dark outside. No one saw the Cuban remove a suitcase from the back of his Cordoba; no one would have remarked on it if they had. He was back in two minutes.

"There is a freighter bound for Puerto Rico. I was on my way to deliver them to someone on the ship who can smuggle them into Cuba. But no matter, I can get more."

Estrada emptied the contents onto the bed.

"Jati-Matics," Bolan said, impressed. There was no mistaking the curiously bent barrel that protruded from its compact receiver.

"Ever use one?"

"No," admitted Bolan. "I've read the test reports. But I haven't had the chance to fire one."

"You one, *señor*, a matched pair!" *Espectro* picked up the nearest one and displayed its virtues. "Smaller than an Uzi and very light. The angled barrel cuts recoil to a minimum. You can empty an entire magazine—forty rounds—with one hand. The silencer is most effective. And you'll find one of the latest laser sights in that case."

Bolan tried on one of the shoulder holsters and slipped his jacket over it. The rig was undetectable.

"First thing in the morning, I have to pay a call on the Feds. We'll rendezvous at lunchtime. You can tell me what you've found out."

"You're moving fast, *señor*."

"It's the only way, *amigo*."

Bolan glanced back at the two Finnish SMGs and nodded with satisfaction.

7

Field camouflage requires breaking up an outline with natural materials or generalized color schemes to escape the eye of an observer. Role camouflage demands the opposite. The cover must be constructed from precise details to withstand close scrutiny.

Don Edelman's well-used Nikon and tape recorder were just such convincing props. Bolan could have bought himself a new camera or a cassette recorder, but it took years of service for the black matte finish to be worn down to the shiny casing in places.

Additional film containers were secured to the shoulder strap with old insulating tape, grimy from the journalist's travels. And the leather satchel that carried the Sanyo recorder had a similarly well-worn look.

Together with Ziman's letter of introduction, Melody Wren, one of the two girls working Reception, bought the Executioner's presentation of himself as Mark Bailey, roving correspondent for *Now* magazine.

She had gone to fetch Captain Bryce. And there was no reason to think he wouldn't swallow Bolan's cover story just as easily.

"I don't think you'll be allowed to take any photographic equipment inside with you, sir," the other girl at the reception desk told him. "But you can leave your equipment here with me."

"Thanks." Bolan unslung the battered Nikon. He read her name tag. Karen Campbell. "I wonder if you could help me, Miss Campbell."

He fished out the photo of Don Edelman aboard the boat. The name *Ropedancer* was painted on her stern. "I'm trying to get in touch with an old friend of mine, a war buddy. This is the last picture I have of him. I thought perhaps while I'm being given the tour you might check through records..."

"I'd be glad to, sir." The receptionist appeared to be grateful to be asked for something other than the directions to the washroom or what time she got off duty.

The man who accompanied Melody Wren back to the reception area was not the Coast Guard officer Bolan was expecting. He was dressed in civilian clothes.

"Mr. Bailey? My name's Leo Webber. I'm the assistant director of investigations. I also act as a kind of liaison officer between the various agencies that make up the Gulf Coast Task Force. I understand you want to write us up for, what was it, *Now* magazine?"

Bolan had given the name of an obscure Canadian newsmagazine—real enough, but less chance that it would be checked up on.

"Always glad to cooperate with the press," Webber assured him as they walked down the long, air-conditioned corridor.

The Federal Gulf Coast Task Force was based on the successful South Florida agency and extended their watch along the northwestern reaches of Florida, past New Orleans and the bayou country, and around to Texas. The

FGCTF had offices in St. Petersburg, and there was a western division headquartered in Houston.

It was composed of select personnel from the DEA, FBI, Coast Guard, Customs Service, Border Patrol and officers from a variety of police drug squads.

"We also have our own legal pool of prosecutors, and judges especially to hear smuggling and peddling cases," Webber finished explaining as he ushered his guest into the intelligence center.

"We've got Betty Blimp working for us," said Webber, jabbing his finger upward. "Eye-in-the-sky. A roving radar balloon. Plus three E-2C Hawkeye mini-AWACs on loan from the Navy. But it's a hell of an area to cover."

Flashing lights blinked out their colored codes across a large wall map of the entire Gulf of Mexico. Computer terminals flickered with long strings of correlated information.

"This helps us monitor the Caribbean choke points—the straits through which most of the boats must pass. We log ship movements and crew listings, especially checking for prior drug convictions. We track small-plane flight plans and those that haven't filed..."

"Looks like a war room to me."

"It is a war, Mr. Bailey. I hope you'll make that clear to your readers. Fifty billion dollars' worth of cocaine is coming through Florida this year. We can't even guess the value of the marijuana being transshipped through this region.

"The DEA has given up trying to project reasonable estimates. It's the biggest business in the United States. Worldwide, the drug dealers' profits are topping the one trillion mark. But we're shouldering our part in this battle. Let's go to my office. I'll show you some reports and the clippings on our most recent busts."

Jacques Terrence was right, Bolan reflected. The Feds were as eager for publicity as any starlet in Hollywood. On the other hand, Bolan knew he was being given only the most superficial tour. Sure, he had been shown more than was open to the public, but not that much more than could be read up in any previous news stories.

"Oh, you're taking care of Mr. Bailey." The Coast Guard officer looked a little put out that his PR function had been usurped by Webber.

"Mark Bailey...this is Captain Bryce." Webber introduced them perfunctorily. "Can't keep the press waiting, Captain. Thought I'd handle it for you."

Bryce touched the peak of his cap and moved off to attend to more pressing business. Webber shrugged behind his back.

"Okay, I can supply you with anything you need," Webber said as he shut the office door. "Statistics, prior news clippings, photographs... Here, maybe you could use this."

He slid a large glossy print across the desk. It was a night shot showing Webber standing in the bow of a launch, gun in one hand and a loud hailer in the other—probably taken at dockside, but it was meant to look as if he was about to stop a boatload of smugglers single-handedly.

There was a framed copy of the same print on the wall alongside a picture of Webber shaking hands with the U.S. Vice-President.

"Do you know anything about a boat called the *Betsy Lou*? It might be missing, even sunk."

Webber shook his head slowly, stiffly. "No, can't say I do. An awful lot of boats go missing these days, Mr. Bailey. Like I said, it's a war."

His denial was unconvincing.

Bolan stood up, careful to pick up Webber's photograph. "Might be able to use this. Thanks. It's all right, I can find my way back to the front desk. I don't want to take up any more of your time. You've got a big war on your hands."

Bolan retraced his steps down the corridor. He crossed to the desk and asked, "Any luck?"

"Yes," Ms Campbell said, handing back the journalist's camera. "Actually, Jim McGuire in our Records section recognized the other man, not your friend though—he's Judd Cooper. Jim says he's always moored the *Ropedancer* in the marina at Bluewater Bay. Here, I jotted down his name and the directions on the back of the photo."

"Thanks. You've been a great help."

"Did you get a good story this morning?"

"I think so, but there are a few more pieces to be researched."

Bolan had spent longer than anticipated listening to Leo Webber. He was running late. He called Pedro Estrada at a prearranged number. "What have you got?"

"Bull Oakum has been twisting arms for Juan Cardona. Oakum's an enforcer for Cardona's drug racket."

"And the woman? Anything on her?"

"Yes. She goes by the name of Amada Madero now. She's turned her artistic talents to designing clothes and has a small chain of boutiques in St. Pete's, Tampa, Clearwater and Sarasota.

"Anyway, you can judge her for yourself. There's going to be a preview of her latest creations on Clearwater Beach this afternoon. A kind of modeling show on Pier 60. It'll take you about an hour to get up there."

"I'm on my way."

THE MIDDAY HEAT WAS OPPRESSIVE. Bolan scowled as the smell of melting tar, burnt rubber and gas fumes assailed his nostrils. At least the traffic thinned out as he headed toward Seminole.

He was glad that he had seen something of the interagency defense network against the drug trade firsthand. Still, with all those satellites and spy planes, radar, Coast Guard cutters on sea patrol, informers and computerized backup, he couldn't help wondering why they had such little real success.

The smugglers were getting some powerful help to run this formidable blockade.

And what about the *Betsy Lou* that Don had so carefully marked on his chart? Despite the formal denial, Bolan was certain that Leo Webber did know something about the boat. What were the Feds keeping to themselves?

Estrada had done well. Somehow Juan Cardona and his hired help, Bull Oakum, tied in with the mystery ship. Bolan was equally sure of that. And whatever Don Edelman had discovered, it was worth killing him for. But had he shared the secret with anyone else? Had he told Judd Cooper?

Bolan felt the missing pieces would fall into place as soon as he had made the acquaintance of Maria Ortega or, as she now styled herself, Amada Madero.

He reached over, slipped one of the cassettes into the borrowed recorder and switched it on. He was listening as he drove past the city limits. A brand-new Buick accelerated to keep up with him.

"I'm not a proud man, my friends. Pride is a sin. I'm begging you to send in a donation to our Word of God Fund. Every cent will go toward building a new and more powerful transmitter. Then more good folks will be able to watch my daily TV show or hear the Good Word on their radios. Just send what you can afford to KRST, here in Alachalafaya...."

It was a moment of eerie coincidence. Bolan had just passed a billboard advertising the opening of Jungle-Land, when he registered the face of Magnus Angell staring down at him.

If it hadn't been for the legend Are You Ready for Your Appointment with the Lord? underneath the portrait, Bolan would not have known he was the evangelist.

Something on the periphery of Bolan's watchfulness had triggered a conscious sweep. He checked both mirrors. The Buick was still behind.

It might have been following him, but now it was drawing alongside as they slowed for the light. A tail would hardly show himself like that.

Bolan looked across at the other car as they stopped.

The window was open. The driver stared back at Bolan with pale, soulless eyes. His mouth tightened in a sneer.

Bolan's mental file instantaneously superimposed the photos that Stuart Farson had shown him.

Gouzenkov!

The Russian raised his hand level with the window. He was holding a P6 silenced pistol aimed at Bolan's face.

8

Bolan reacted instinctively. He slammed the gas pedal to the floor, gunning the car toward the intersection.

The bullet from Gouzenkov's gun embedded itself uselessly in a palm tree—there was only empty space where Bolan's car had been.

The Executioner veered in front of a delivery truck, turned a sharp left and then, to avoid a squeeze play with a bus, fishtailed into the wrong lane.

A startled tourist, seeing the speeding car coming at him head-on, only had time to swerve for the safety of a shopping-mall entrance.

The front right hubcap went spinning as Bolan's vehicle hit the median, leaped over the low hump and landed in front of the surprised bus driver.

The light behind had changed. In his side mirror Bolan caught a glimpse of the frustrated assassin trying to cut across two lanes of traffic in an effort to follow his quarry.

Bolan hung a right, but not fast enough to fool the Russian.

The Buick had turned onto Bolan's trail.

The Executioner spent a moment considering his options. Fight or flight? Duel it out with Gouzenkov on the back streets of Clearwater, or somehow lose him? The opportunity to stage an encounter with the Cuban woman was too good to pass up. He'd have to shake the killer.

Screeching tires scattered palm debris as Bolan turned hard again. He was northbound, approaching the sleepy downtown core. The lights were with him as he sped past Fort Harrison.

He continued on for three more blocks.

Gouzenkov had risked running a red to catch up. There were no cops in sight.

Bolan signaled right, but then abruptly turned left down the hill past the park. He hit the horn to warn a group of elderly music lovers leaving a lunchtime concert. Even in the heat of this chase, Bolan's concern was that no innocent bystanders get hurt.

This was a private war.

He swung up onto the bridge approach. It was right on the hour. A tall-masted sloop was waiting to go through. The causeway bridgemaster hit the flashing red lights.

Bolan gunned the engine. His wheels drummed on the open grating as he raced across the bridge.

The black-and-white barrier was dropping as Bolan flashed past.

The bridge began to open, stranding the Russian assassin on the other side.

Bolan had guessed right. Gouzenkov might have tried to hit him at a stoplight and raced away but, until his mission was completed, he could not afford to face the awkward questions that might have arisen from a traffic violation. That ounce of inhibition had cost him the chase—this time.

Bolan was grateful for the brief reprieve as he drove along the crowded beachfront, looking for a place to park. He found a spot about two minutes' walk from the front.

A large white marquee had been set up on the sand at the foot of the pier. A couple of suntanned cops, both wearing mirrored lenses, kept curious onlookers from barging into this temporary dressing room.

Most of the spectators were packed around the roped-off runway, watching the models strut and twirl as they showed off Amada Madero's latest collection of beachwear.

It did not take Bolan long to locate Estrada. He was admiring a long-legged blonde displaying an après-swim lounger.

A slim young man holding a cordless mike announced, "And now Nicole will show us a delightful..."

"That's Sandy Martin," Estrada told Bolan, indicating the MC. "He's actually the general manager for Amada's chain of boutiques."

Bolan watched the announcer lift the cape off Nicole's shoulders as she swept past, leaving the model free to exhibit her charms in the briefest of blue-green bikinis. It was a stunning symphony of shimmering turquoise on copper skin.

"A miracle of engineering," Estrada muttered.

"The swimwear?" Bolan pretended to check the focus on the Nikon.

"Er, of course."

Bolan chuckled at Estrada's transparent lie. "So tell me, how does a penniless refugee wind up with a business like this?"

Estrada turned his back on the models before he replied.

"Soon after her arrival here she attracted the attention of Manuel Rivas. He could afford the lawyers to smooth out the immigration process. She even changed her name legally. Rivas was a powerful man. He had many interests, from construction to fast-food franchises, cigar manufacturing to the garment industry."

"So he bankrolled his new girlfriend?"

"I did not say she was his girlfriend, *señor*. He was an older man, much older. More of a father figure to Amada. A man could be satisfied just to be seen with this woman by his side."

"Did he have Mob connections?"

"I think Rivas straddled the borderline. Many people have links deep in the underworld without being gangsters themselves." Estrada looked knowingly at the big American. "Rivas must have had a conscience because when his junior partner wanted to capitalize on the growing cocaine business, the old man flatly refused. The partner's name was Juan Cardona."

A tingle ran through Bolan. He was getting closer. The pieces were fitting together.

"There was a split. Not long afterward Rivas got in his car one morning, turned the key, and…boom! Some said it was because of a union dispute, but most suspected Cardona. Nothing was ever proven."

"But Amada Madero kept her clothing business."

"*Sí.* And not only that. She inherited Rivas's mansion here in Harbor Oaks. I drove past it on the way to the beach." The Cuban's expressive eyebrows showed how impressed he had been. "Cardona got most everything else. Or he just took it over. Everything that is, except the one thing he wanted most…."

"Amada Madero herself."

"Right. My informants tell me that Cardona has never given up wanting her. My eyes tell me this is true. See over there, by the soft-drink stand? Those two hoods are Cardona's men. He offers her his constant protection even if she wants nothing to do with him."

"Unwelcome bodyguards or spies? Presumably they report her every movement to Cardona. And that of anyone who comes near her."

"Of course, *señor*. Cardona is a jealous man. If he can't have Amada, well, who else would be foolish enough to make a play for her with those goons hanging around?"

"Does she contribute to the cause? She must be rich now. And she has every reason to hate Castro and his crew."

"That's how I came across her," confessed Estrada. "A friend of mine—he has his own group in Tampa—approached her for funds. But she will have nothing to do with the resistance movement."

"Where is she now?" Bolan swept the sea of faces through the single-lens reflex.

"At this moment, she is to your left," Estrada announced quite matter-of-factly. "About thirty yards away. Wearing the pale blue blouse. Standing by the corner of the tent."

There were many beautiful women at the Pier 60 show: graceful fashion correspondents, some cute vacationers and, of course, the eye-catching models themselves, but in Bolan's judgment not one of them was in the same league as Amada Madero.

She stood serenely apart from the swirling ebb and flow of the afternoon's business. Her calm bearing seemed self-assured, her dark eyes were almost too big for that delicate oval face, and despite the humidity, her lustrous hair was perfectly groomed.

Manuel Rivas had been a fortunate man indeed. And it was no wonder that Juan Cardona wanted her so badly.

Bolan tore his eyes away to sector-scan the throng. Once he thought he caught a glimpse of the Spetsnaz killer, but the straw mop belonged to a beach bum and not the ace from Strakhov's sleeve. There were too many cameramen and cops around for Gouzenkov to make another play in public.

"You wait here," Bolan instructed Estrada. "Keep an eye on Cardona's muscle."

He plunged through the crowd. The models were posing for a final group portrait. The onlookers were applauding. And Sandy Martin was wrapping the show. "Ladies and gentlemen, thank you all for coming to view the new Madero collection. There will be another showing on Friday at JungleLand, the Suncoast's newest attraction.. "

AMADA MADERO WAS RELIEVED. The first public unveiling of her latest designs had gone well. She opened her purse and extracted a thin cigarette wrapped in dark brown paper.

A huge fist proffered a lighter under her nose.

The woman ignored the offer, rummaging around in her bag. She did not look up at the newcomer.

"You certainly staged an attractive display, Miss Madero," a deep voice said. Finally she gave up the search for a light and thrust her head forward to fire the smoke.

"I hope you got some good pictures," she replied, indicating the stranger's equipment. "We have tried to provide an interesting photo opportunity."

"What I would like is the opportunity to meet the woman behind the clothes."

She was still wary but now slightly amused, whether at his persistence or the hint of a double meaning in his request.

This man was not the usual hanger-on to be found at the fringes of the fashion world. For one thing, he was undeniably a man. All man.

"Could we get away from this crowd? Perhaps talk awhile."

Sandy Martin, seeing some guy pestering his boss, moved protectively toward her. Amada gently waved him away. He looked thankful he was not going to have to order the big man to leave.

"What do you really want, Mr....?"

"Bailey. Mark Bailey." Bolan lied easily. "I'm not really a fashion photographer. But I am interested in doing a story on Cuban-Americans who have found success here."

"Like your friend over there." She nodded in the direction of Estrada. Bolan was surprised. So, Estrada had caught her eye already.

Bolan was about to follow through, but Amada turned away defensively. "There is no story in my work, Mr. Bailey, beyond what you see."

"Well, at least let's have a drink and talk it over. Everything will be strictly off the record."

Amada began to walk back to her car.

Bolan fell in beside her.

She looked up shyly at the handsome profile of her escort. She was torn between an impulsive attraction toward this stranger and a wary caution to preserve her privacy.

Amada saw Cardona's two thugs lounging against a shop window. She moved a little closer to her escort, feeling secure with this man by her side.

They just had to make their presence felt. They had to let the newcomer know he was not welcome. It was how they made their living.

The one with a scar at the corner of his mouth straightened, moving a pace out onto the sidewalk so that Bolan would have to step aside or bump into him. The second dude closed in, too, casually reaching into his jacket pocket.

Bolan did not move over. He stopped in front of Scarlip. Amada was already safely past them.

Scarlip wanted to step back for room to give Bolan a shove. He couldn't budge. Bolan had suddenly jammed his foot down hard on Scarlip's toes. Then the Executioner's fist shot out like a piston—a short, lethally powerful body-blow sunk into Scarlip's solar plexus. The hardman could manage nothing more than a strangled wheeze.

The second heavy made his play. Bolan's other hand snaked out and wrapped over the other guy's pocket. He began to crush the fingers he could feel nursing a snub-nosed special.

"Back off. Or I'll make you pull that trigger," he growled.

Scarlip's buddy opened his eyes wide in pain and utter fear, then mutely nodded. This bastard was about to make him blow his own balls off.

"Move on, scum, or next time you'll be a soprano."

The two hoods scurried away. Scarlip was cursing under each heaving breath.

Even to the closest passerby it hardly appeared that so much as a scuffle had taken place, so quietly and methodically had Bolan dispatched the problem.

Amada Madero had been about to take advantage of Bolan's momentary engagement to slip away. Instead she now waited by her car. No one had ever dealt with Cardona's men that way. This man was proving as intriguing as he was attractive.

"Mr. Bailey, I think I'll take you up on that drink."

9

The morning was bright. The road was busy. Bolan checked the mirror repeatedly on his drive south to Bluewater Bay.

He had good reason to be doubly cautious now. Gouzenkov was still somewhere out there dogging his trail, waiting to strike. And without even meeting the man, Bolan had made a powerful enemy in Juan Cardona. Although the big soldier's automatic alarm systems were on full alert, he found it possible to dwell pleasurably on the night before.

Amada Madero had been as charming as she was beautiful. She had probed, she had teased, she had candidly appealed to him. Exactly who was Mark Bailey?

Did he work for the government? Officials of various agencies had approached her before. She would not give anything away.

Was he involved with one of the expatriate organizations? She loved Cuba but she could not become involved with a hopeless cause.

Was he a rival to Cardona? She wanted nothing to do with the underworld.

Bolan convinced her on every count that he did not represent any of those interests. But she had not been won over sufficiently to drop her guard.

She had refused to talk about her background except in vague generalities. It was as if her life had begun here in Florida as Amada Madero, fashion designer and businesswoman.

Each knew the other was concealing a secret past, but the sheer pleasure of the present was worth holding on to...drinks led to dinner, and then to a late nightcap.

She had still not broken Bolan's cover, just as he had not yet fully penetrated her defenses. They had not even decided if they were destined to be friends or foes, only that there was an undercurrent of sensual excitement between them, a powerful attraction that would be foolish to deny.

He had escorted her home to Harbor Oaks. Estrada was right to have been impressed. It was a white-colonnaded mansion built by old Southern money, with a guarded driveway that would not have disgraced the home of a movie superstar. Manuel Rivas had provided generously for his protégée.

Bolan had left her at the front entrance, but he took with him an open invitation to return...and the memory of the warmest, softest lips. He could still taste her on his mouth.

A green-and-white road sign interrupted Bolan's reverie. The next two exits led to Bluewater Bay. The road behind was clear as Bolan slowed down for the ramp.

The sand-pine scrub had been leveled to a strip of lots no bigger than postage stamps for a land-hungry developer. Only a few cabbage palms had been left at strategic intervals to provide a tropical atmosphere.

Even the beautiful beach was now polluted with decaying heaps of seaweed—overdredging had altered the natural currents of the bay.

The men who did these things were criminals; not the kind the Executioner pursued with single-minded diligence, but criminals nonetheless. Florida was being choked to ecological death.

Bolan parked in the municipal lot by the marina. Kids were casting nets from the dock. One of the youngsters shook out a pinfish from his net and told Bolan where to find the *Ropedancer*. Judd Cooper had moved his boat down to Ward's Yard.

Bolan left the car right outside the gates. The boat-yard was deserted, but a faded sign told him the *Rope-dancer* was for hire for fishing, diving or sight-seeing trips around the bay.

He walked past a weathered lobster boat, its seams drying out beyond repair as it slowly baked apart on the cradle. The *Ropedancer* was moored at the far end of Ward's dock. Bolan approached it from the same angle as the photo had been taken.

A compressor and some diving gear cluttered the aft deck, although the *Ropedancer* was obviously maintained with a loving hand. At that moment it appeared as deserted as the yard.

"Anyone aboard?" Bolan shouted.

No reply.

He jumped down onto the deck and repeated his inquiry. But still no one answered.

The catch on the cabin door was open. Bolan pushed it back and peered inside.

He climbed down the three wooden steps into the interior. The layout was comfortably crowded and there was ample evidence that Judd Cooper lived aboard full-time.

Bolan moved forward. Despite the undisturbed jumble of clothes, charts and breakfast things, Bolan sensed that something was wrong. There was someone else aboard. A warning tingle at the base of his skull triggered reflexive action.

He spun just as the man stepped out of the head, a heavy wrench clasped in his upraised fist. Bolan grabbed the attacker's wrist before he could find room to swing, and pushed the assailant back against the bulkhead.

"Hold it! You're Judd Cooper, aren't you?"

The sailor still struggled to free himself from the Executioner's iron grip. He wouldn't confess his identity, Bolan knew, but he recognized the man well enough from the picture. He did not want to hurt the guy. He shook loose the wrench. "Look, I'm a friend of Don Edelman's. I just want to talk with you."

Cooper backed down.

Bolan released his hold and stepped away.

"Friend of Don's, you say?" The skipper rubbed his wrist. "You the fellow he was going to call in New York?"

"Yeah, I'm the one. Mack Bolan."

They shook hands.

"Don spoke of you a few times. And always with respect. He was proud to know you." Cooper picked up the wrench and threw it back in his toolbox. "Want a drink? I guess I owe you one."

"Sure," Bolan agreed, just to be sociable. "Tell me, Judd, do you always greet strangers that way?"

"No. It's not my style. But then you could tell that," chuckled Cooper. He had to move the morning paper to retrieve a glass tumbler. The boatman shook his head.

"Damn shame what happened to Don. I told him not to get involved."

He swiveled the newspaper so that his guest could read the short follow-up piece on the front of the local section.

"Went down to the store this morning to top up my supplies and when I came back I saw someone snooping around the boat. He took off in a skiff before I could get back to her," Cooper offered by way of explanation for his hostile attempt to crack Bolan's skull. "Looked mean...built like a bull."

"That's what they call him," said Bolan. "Bull Oakum."

"Here." Cooper put the whiskey down on the newspaper and again shook his head sadly. "Damn shame. I told Don to back off. Give it to the authorities, I said, let them handle it. Even gave him the name of someone I knew on the Drug Task Force. But he wouldn't go that route. Don said it wouldn't do any good."

"I'm beginning to think he's right." Bolan didn't touch his drink—it was too early—but he watched Cooper toss his back and pour a second shot. "Tell me, just what did Don find?"

Cooper said nothing. He stared moodily as the breezes ruffled the water's surface into crosscut ripples.

"It's about the *Betsy Lou*, isn't it?" Bolan prompted.

The skipper made no reply at first, just rasped a hand across his stubbled chin. And then—maybe it was the drink that loosened his tongue, or maybe it was Bolan's mention of the sunken boat—the story started to come out in a rush.

"Aye, the *Betsy Lou*. It's about that and more. Don was writing a book about the treasure hunters. Done a bit of salvage work myself. That's how he and I met. I put him on to a few people. Sometimes ran him out to watch them at work, see if they were finding anything. Most of them needed the publicity—it's an expensive business— and they trusted that Don wouldn't give away any real secrets. You know, precise coordinates of the search patterns, that sort of thing.''

"You say he got on well with most of the treasure divers," commented Bolan, "but did he run afoul of any of them?"

"Alex Grogan, maybe...but then Grogan doesn't like anybody.'' Bolan studied Cooper's weathered features. It was clear from his expression that he did not care much for Grogan, either. "Don got this radio equipment. He used to call up the operators or the mag boats and find out how things were progressing. I think it made him feel like part of the hunt.

"Anyway, one night, oh, about a month ago, he picks up a Mayday from a big cruiser called the *Betsy Lou*. It had run into bad weather and was shipping water fast. Then a couple of days later we hear that Alex Grogan found the skipper adrift, picked him up and brought him into Key West. No one else was saved, just Clem Bodine.''

"Lucky man."

"You don't know how lucky. According to Don's calculations Grogan shouldn't have been anywhere near the last radioed position of the *Betsy Lou*. For months he'd been searching for the *Saint Christopher* off Ragged Rocks Cay...''

It only took a second for Bolan to reach the obvious alternative. "Or the other way around. The *Betsy Lou* was nowhere near her reported position."

"Right. But if a captain starts to broadcast a Mayday signal, why does he give a false position?"

"Maybe he wanted to scuttle his boat where no one else would find her until he was ready to salvage her himself," Bolan guessed. "Still, he'd be taking quite a risk that he'd be picked up by someone. Did Don contact this Bodine character?"

"Tried to, but it was too late. Bodine was found stabbed to death in an alleyway behind a bar in Key West."

"So there were no known survivors of the *Betsy Lou* in the end."

"No, and only Grogan knows where he picked up Clem Bodine."

"But unless Bodine told him, Grogan can't know for sure where the boat went down."

"Aye, but there isn't a man better equipped to find her. That's his business."

"Okay, let's suppose her cargo was drugs—cocaine, most likely—Bodine may have taken advantage of the bad weather, used it as an excuse to scuttle the boat. The buyers wouldn't pay him off for the trip, but to them a lost boat is just another business expense. Meanwhile, Bodine planned to go back later and retrieve the payload for himself."

"That's what Don reckoned, too. He did a lot of figuring. Currents, wind speed, likely drift, track of the storm that supposedly sunk the *Betsy Lou*... Far as he could tell she went down near Dogleg Bank."

"Where is that?"

Judd Cooper reached across for one of the rolled-up charts. He cleared away the newspaper and glasses and smoothed out the map with work-worn hands, anchoring the corner of the paper with a flare pistol.

His fingertip traced a passage through the Keys, turning into the Straits of Florida, until he reached the depth contour that led past the Ragged Rocks to Dogleg Bank.

"Here. But everyone who knows these waters calls it Hammerhead Reef."

Cooper's finger tapped down on the exact spot that Don had marked on his chart.

"And you know those waters?"

"Sure. Good spot for fishing, especially if you're after shark."

"How much could she have been carrying?"

The skipper shrugged but took a guess anyway. "On a boat that size you could stash, oh, maybe five hundred keys."

"And that would have a street value of anywhere from two to four hundred million dollars."

Bolan's thoughts were racing. No wonder Webber had denied all knowledge of the *Betsy Lou*. The Federal drug authorities must have been looking for it themselves, and they would not want journalists, amateur investigators or sport divers getting in the way.

For the amount of money involved the buyers, too, would want to retrieve their cargo. But unless Clem Bodine talked before he was killed—maybe he wouldn't, thought Bolan, and that's why he was knifed—then they could be searching the wrong area for weeks before being reasonably certain they had been double-crossed.

And how close was Alex Grogan to finding the *Betsy Lou*? He would go after it, for sure. It was too big a temptation to pass up. Cooper's next comment echoed Bolan's own thoughts.

"It's worth a whole lot more than a treasure hunter could hope to salvage in a lifetime," he noted. "That's if you don't mind tangling with the likes of the Cruz brothers or Cardona's gang. Me, I steer clear of drugs."

Where were the drugs bound for, wondered Bolan, and who had commissioned Clem Bodine to make the run? He'd lay odds on Juan Cardona.

"The more Don looked into that whole sorry subject, the more he thought there might be a book in it," Cooper said. "One evening he showed up here all excited like, tells me he's made a big discovery...figured out how they ran the blockade. But he wouldn't give me the details."

"Perhaps you're lucky he didn't."

"I guess so. Anyway, we talked late that night, finished a bottle or two, that's when I told him to take what he had to the Feds."

"But Don suspected he had a reason for not trusting even them."

Bolan mulled that over. Whom had Don been in contact with when he was trying to figure out the mysterious sinking of the *Betsy Lou* for himself? His investigation had alerted someone, someone who had put Cardona on to him.

One thing seemed sure. When Don had invited Bolan to Florida he had signed his own death warrant, but Bolan had arrived at his house and disturbed Bull Oakum before he had the chance to seize Don's calculations and chart work for his boss.

There was only one place to start unraveling this mess and that was under at least twenty feet of water out on Hammerhead Reef.

Cooper was staring at his empty glass. "Yep, it looked as if Don planned to bust it all wide open in a book.

Meanwhile everybody's looking for the *Betsy Lou*—the Coast Guard and all those other Feds, the smugglers who got cheated, Alex Grogan...finders keepers!''

"How long would it take us to get to Hammerhead Reef?" Bolan asked.

Judd Cooper looked away, staring out at the water, not believing that Bolan was serious. There was a pause before he answered.

"Seven hours. Six, if the weather holds."

"Well, you're for hire, aren't you? That's what the sign says." Bolan pulled out a roll of currency notes. "We could be there before dark."

Cooper scratched his jaw. His eyes settled on the newspaper again. "Put your money away, mister. I'll go for Don's sake or not at all."

"Then we're both going for the same reason."

10

"*Carrera de Indias*, the Spaniards called it—their highway to the Indies," Judd Cooper explained as the *Ropedancer* cut a frothy wake through the gunmetal blue of the sea. "It's the maritime road followed by the galleons taking jewels, silver and gold bullion back to the coffers of Spain."

Bolan noticed the rapture on the man's face. It was obvious that out here Cooper was in his natural element. He seemed younger, tougher, more exhilarated. The low dark humps of the keys were left strung out across the horizon behind them as the *Ropedancer* sought the deeper, safer waters of the Gulf Stream.

Bolan sucked in the bracing salt air. He watched as a gull swooped low to check them out, circled twice, then headed for the easy pickings from the fishing boats cruising between the reefs and far-off keys.

Dozens of boats dotted the waters off this southeasternmost tip of the States. This was one of the busiest areas in the world for pleasure craft of every kind.

Maybe Clem Bodine had not taken such a foolhardy gamble after all, Bolan figured, for with a well-stocked inflatable raft there was a chance that he would be picked up by someone sooner or later. In fact the farther he drifted, the more easily he might have got away with the false position he claimed for the *Betsy Lou*.

Bodine's plan started to come unstuck when Grogan picked him up so quickly.

"There's Tom Greaves! See—the *Lucky Lady*—off the starboard beam," Cooper called out from the wheel. "Probably taking a bunch of tourists out to snorkel around the old *Buen Jesus*. You know, Greaves has been luckier than most at the game, but he still has to spend more time acting out the role of treasure diver than actually going down for the stuff. Yessir, it's a costly business, all right."

The *Lucky Lady* veered away to the southwest and was soon lost from sight. A first-time sailor might have thought it rough out here, but it was quite a calm afternoon for the straits.

The *Ropedancer* was cutting across the waves at an angle. Every sixth or seventh wave was big enough to lift her bow so that she slid over the crest. Then the hull slithered down through the following trough as Cooper pushed them onward. And the big GMC diesel filled the boat with a dull, persistent throbbing.

"Where was the *Betsy Lou* coming from?" Bolan asked as he served the skipper a mug of hot coffee.

"Don found out that Bodine had originally sailed from Grand Turk. If the drugs came from Cuba, and that's what he reckoned, then my guess is that the *Betsy Lou* rendezvoused with a mother ship somewhere off the Old Bahama Channel, took his cargo aboard, then deviated just enough from the obvious course home to scuttle her on Hammerhead."

Bolan took his coffee down to the cabin to study the charts again, then he rested awhile to conserve his energy for whatever lay ahead.

Over the years Bolan had developed the invaluable ability to recharge his batteries from stolen catnaps, even under the most unlikely circumstances.

He drifted to sleep wondering how Estrada's investigation was progressing. The Cuban was using his contacts on both sides of the law to probe the full extent of Cardona's drug empire. He might uncover a direct connection to the *Betsy Lou*.

An internal clock nudged Bolan awake shortly before their ETA at Hammerhead Reef. But Cooper had not called out yet, nor had he slackened speed.

Bolan reheated the coffee and lit a cigarette. The chart was a patchwork of arrows, dotted lines, soundings and exotic names. Grogan had had at least three weeks' head start to crisscross this area, but there was still a mighty lot of ocean to be searched.

He turned to the newspaper. The follow-up story on Don's crash added nothing to what he already knew. Peter Ziman was quoted as saying that Don Edelman's untimely death would be a tragic loss to his many fans. Yeah, thought Bolan, and to your commission account.

He scanned through the Sports section and, as he was leafing through the local pages for a second time, a captioned photo caught his eye. It was a shot of a young woman cutting the ribbon at an opening ceremony, but there was no mistaking who she was...he had already seen her picture on the wall of Leo Webber's office.

''Melissa Cuts the Tape!'' read the copy underneath.

Mrs. Melissa Webber, Magnus Angell's youngest daughter, cuts the ribbon to open her father's new broadcasting complex at Alachalafaya. The well-known evangelist said the powerful transmitter will help him bring the Good Word to thousands more viewers and listeners in the Southeast.

The tingle was back—an ominous certainty this time—as Bolan felt the puzzle falling into place and now pulling clearly into focus. So, Leo Webber was Magnus Angell's son-in-law. Cozy. It was all in the family....

"We're too late, Mack!" shouted Cooper. "Looks like Grogan has beaten us to it."

Bolan leaped up the companionway and stood behind Cooper in the wheelhouse. Apart from a line of boiling waves that marked the sudden shallows of the reef, it looked like any other stretch of tropic water.

"Well, he sure ain't looking for the *Saint Christopher* this far out," said Cooper. "This here's the Dogleg Bank."

Grogan's boat had seen service in a dozen different guises before he acquired her and refitted her for diving and salvage work. The *Engracia* was about one hundred twenty feet long, painted flat black, with rust-streaked hawsepipes and plywood sheets wired down over missing portholes. It looked as if Grogan could use an infusion of capital. Anchored fore and aft to prevent her from drifting onto the reef, the *Engracia* looked more like a derelict than a treasure hunter's flagship.

Most of the crew were on the afterdeck checking out their diving gear. Two more were securing a twenty-seven-foot boat to the *Engracia*'s platform. One of the men shouted and pointed to the approaching *Ropedancer*.

As Bolan checked each detail through Cooper's binoculars, a motorized raft suddenly surged around the stern and plowed toward them. Bolan got a glimpse of a sun-bleached head.

"The welcoming committee," Cooper grunted. "You want to go below?"

"Uh-huh. I'll keep out of sight," Bolan said. He ducked back into the stairwell.

He could hear the waspish buzz of the outboard over the well-muffled chugging of the *Ropedancer*'s engines.

"Hello, Judd! What are you doing out here?"

"Might ask you the same thing, Suddick. You working for Grogan these days?"

"He pays well," shouted the other man, bringing the rubber craft closer alongside the *Ropedancer*. "So what brings you out to Hammerhead?"

"Taking another high roller out after shark—insists on catching the big one. Don't they all?" There was a convincing weariness to Cooper's remarks. It was a situation both men were familiar with.

"Where is he now?" called out Suddick.

"Below. Still sleeping off his lunchtime martinis. You know how they are."

The young diver laughed at that. He maneuvered the inflatable closer. "You want to come aboard, see what we've found?"

Cooper gave a fleeting glance back over his shoulder. Bolan shook his head emphatically. They might never get off again…and the *Ropedancer* would then join the *Betsy Lou* in her watery grave.

"No. Gotta take this fellow in soon. Catching a flight back to Cleveland tonight."

Suddick shrugged. "In that case Alex wants you to stand clear. In fact, it would be better if you went fishing someplace else."

Cooper signaled that he got the message.

"I'm on my way," he said. Cooper put the wheel over, waited till the inflatable was safely clear, then opened up. The *Ropedancer* peeled away from the diving site.

Bolan emerged as they left the *Engracia* behind. "Have they found the *Betsy Lou*?"

"Grogan's located something, all right. He had marker buoys down."

"Yeah, and they were getting ready for a deep dive...or a long one. I spotted a battery of diving lights."

"I saw them, too," Cooper said. "Can't believe Grogan would order his men over the side this late in the afternoon for anything other than the *Betsy Lou*. I wouldn't go under after dark out here for the richest treasure ship."

Bolan looked at his watch, then at the sun. It was beginning to streak the sky to the west with pastel shades of russet, pink and lilac, turning the cloud banks into wispy displays of gaudy cotton fluff. He lit a cigarette as he pondered his next move.

He knew he had to go down there, darkness or not. All the necessary equipment was on board. He'd already checked that out.

"At night—say an hour or two before dawn—how close could you get us to the *Engracia*?"

"She's carrying radar. But it was fitted so quickly and carelessly that those radio masts and the smokestack should create quite a shadow off her starboard quarter."

Cooper ran through the problems of such an approach. "If I drifted with the current along the edge of the reef, I guess we could get within two thousand yards. Maybe less. The shoals are treacherous. There's not going to be much of a moon and the clouds will help."

"That's all the edge I need," Bolan said.

COOPER LACED A STEAMING MUG of coffee with whiskey, poured a neat shot for himself, then looked at Bolan. "Time for you to get ready."

Bolan dressed in a full wet suit. The water temperature near the surface was eighty-two, but a long swim would soon begin to take its toll in body warmth.

He strapped on the diving knife. Cooper had wiled away their evening wait, honing the blade to razor sharpness. The Executioner double-checked the regulator, hoisted the tank to his shoulders, picked up the flippers and joined Cooper back in the wheelhouse. The veteran seaman handed him the glasses.

"Looks like they're still hard at it."

Bolan could just make out an eerie luminescence that underlit the surface near the stern-anchor chain. A couple of shadowy figures hurried to the railing as a large net sack was winched aboard.

"I don't think they've spotted us. They're too busy." The *Ropedancer* was riding the swells easily. Cooper had got them in closer than he had hoped. "Let yourself drift in slowly and keep a close watch, I might need you in a hurry."

"Good luck, Mack," the older seaman said. He gestured toward the transmitter. "Any problems and I'm calling in the Coast Guard."

DYNAMITE OFFER

4 EXPLOSIVE NOVELS PLUS SUNGLASSES FREE

delivered right to your home
with no obligation to buy — ever

TAKE 'EM FREE

4 action-packed novels and a rugged pair of sunglasses

With an offer like this, how can you lose?

Return the attached card, and we'll send you 4 adventure novels just like the one you're reading plus a pair of sunglasses — ABSOLUTELY FREE.

If you like them, we'll send you 6 books every other month to preview. Always before they're available in stores. Always for less than the retail price. Always with the right to cancel and owe nothing.

NON-STOP HIGH-VOLTAGE ACTION

As a Gold Eagle subscriber, you'll get the fast-paced, hard-hitting action you crave. Razor-edge stories stripped to their lean muscular essentials. Written in a no-holds-barred style that keeps you riveted from cover to cover.

In addition you'll receive...

- our free newsletter AUTOMAG with every shipment
- special books to preview free and buy at a deep discount

RUSH YOUR ORDER TO US TODAY

Don't let this bargain get away. Send for your 4 free books and sunglasses now. They're yours to keep even if you never buy another Gold Eagle book.

Mean up your act with these tough sunglasses

Unbeatable! That's the word for these tough street-smart shades. Durable metal frame. Scratch-resistant acrylic lenses. Fold 'em into a zip pouch and tuck 'em in your pocket. Best of all, they're yours free.

FREE BOOKS & SUNGLASSES

YEAH, send my 4 **free** Gold Eagle novels plus my **free** sunglasses. Then send me 6 brand-new Gold Eagle novels (2 **Mack Bolans** and one each of **Phoenix Force, Able Team, Track** and **SOBs**) every second month as they come off the presses. Bill me at the low price of $2.25 each (for a total of $13.50 per shipment — a saving of $1.50 off the retail price). There are no shipping, handling or other hidden charges. I can always return a shipment and cancel at any time. Even if I never buy a book from Gold Eagle, the 4 free books and the sunglasses (a $6.95 value) are mine to keep.

166 CIM PAGW

NAME _____

ADDRESS _____ APT. _____

CITY _____

STATE _____ZIP_____

Offer limited to one per household and not valid for present subscribers. Prices subject to change.

PRINTED IN U.S.A

JOIN FORCES WITH GOLD EAGLE'S HEROES

- Mack Bolan...lone crusader against the Mafia and KGB
- Able Team...3-man combat squad blitzes global terrorism
- Phoenix Force...5 mercenaries battle international crime
- Track...weapons genius stalks madman around the world
- SOBs...avengers of justice from Vietnam to Iran

For free offer, detach and mail

Bolan sat on the hatch cover and secured his flippers, bit down on the mouthpiece, then lowered himself quietly over the side.

The velvety coolness of the water smothered him. He took his bearing from the luminous wrist compass and kicked out, each powerful stroke propelling him closer to the *Engracia*.

Bolan counted each stroke as he swam steadily toward his target. He broke through the glinting vault of the surface once to recheck his line of approach. Satisfied that he was right on course, he jackknifed into deeper, colder water as he closed in.

A faint spectral glow ahead of him suddenly grew brighter. It silhouetted a dark bank of jagged rocks dead ahead. Bolan paddled carefully to this natural vantage point.

A battery of high-intensity diving lights illuminated the white hulk of the *Betsy Lou*. She was wedged bow down in a deep fissure. In heavy seas, Clem Bodine had botched his scuttling job. The smuggler's boat was now caught in a V-shaped notch under thirty-five feet of water, barely missing the shallow outer shelf of the reef.

Grogan's divers were taking every precaution. If they upset the precarious balance of the *Betsy Lou*, their prize would slide down into the forbidding darkness of the trench beyond.

They were far too preoccupied with the dangerous task at hand to notice the faint trace of bubbles at the outer fringe of the lighting.

One diver, having gingerly extracted a plastic-wrapped bundle from the bilges, came topside to hand the illicit treasure to the next man. He in turn swam back with it to the third frogman, Suddick, to judge from his mane of sun-bleached hair, who placed it securely within a large netting pouch.

The carrier returned to the wreck to wait for the next packet to be recovered.

Bolan edged closer, staying behind the coral crests of the rock pile. At any moment the lights might reveal the glittering stream of bubbles and mark him as surely as the other swimmers.

A dark shape swooped down from above, arrowing in toward the trespasser. A fourth diver had been circling, ready to ward off any inquisitive marauders of the deep.

He'd found one—Bolan!

The patrolling diver carried a spear gun. He swam as close as he dared, aimed the weapon and fired.

Bolan barely had time to roll to one side as the barbed point grazed a coral fern and lodged itself in a crevice near his outstretched hand.

He seized the line and dragged down hard. Grogan's man had not expected that move. The empty speargun was still secured by a wrist strap. He grappled for his knife even as the intruder pulled him closer.

Bolan grabbed his arm and they tumbled behind the sheltering rocks. In the dim chill twilight the diver struggled for the advantage. Months of swimming for Grogan's team had put him in excellent shape, but he wasn't in the battle-hardened condition of the Executioner.

Justice proved more than a match for greed.

The guard was an amateur, lacking the killer instinct of the professional warrior. He managed to drag his arm upward; the knife blade wavered in front of Bolan's mask. But the Executioner was quicker. He stabbed sideways through the momentarily exposed ribs. Once, twice...the man's lifeblood leaked out in an inky cloud.

Swimming in a half circle, his body gliding over the contours of the rocks, Bolan approached the net man from behind. Suddick had no idea that Death hovered at his shoulder.

The second frogman was still paddling in place over the wreck, waiting for his buddy to reappear with the next bag of coke.

With one slice of his knife, Bolan ripped open Suddick's air tubes. There was an explosion of bubbles, and the man thrashed out wildly with his legs. Bolan gripped Suddick's tank, forced him down, then grasped the slack cable and wrapped a double loop around the diver's neck.

Bolan saw the line go taut and he knew the men on deck assumed it was the signal to winch in another load.

Still twitching spasmodically, Suddick was being hanged underwater by his own workmates. His body was dragged toward the surface.

The guy at the stern of the *Betsy Lou* was alerted by the disturbance behind him. The lights reflected off his faceplate as he looked around. The two men stared at each other across a ghostly arena.

A great silver-white flash arched above them and a gigantic hammerhead, no doubt attracted by the blood of the first dead diver, swept in for an unexpected meal.

One moment Suddick was dangling from the net cable, the next, only his head, shoulders and part of his tattered rib cage were still secured to the rope. The lower half of his body had been torn away in one voracious gulp.

The monstrous fish—Bolan guessed its weight at more than twelve hundred pounds—streaked away with Suddick's entrails still dribbling from its mouth.

The horrified diver was distracted for a second longer than Bolan. By the time he had recovered, the Executioner was upon him with all the force of a fighting shark and a blade that was every bit as sharp as the hammerhead's teeth.

Bolan slashed through the man's suit. More blood clouded the water. The treasure diver buckled forward trying to hold himself together.

More sharks—tigers, mako and smaller hammerheads—were surging forward, maddened by the scent of blood. They began tearing at one another as the frenzy mounted.

The big one was coming back for a second pass.

Bolan felt desperate fingers clutch tight around his ankle. The last diver had emerged from the wreck, saw what was happening, and was now frantically fighting for his life.

Bolan looped over and tried to stab, but Grogan's man caught his wrist. Locked together, they tumbled backward in slow motion onto the crazily tilted deck of the *Betsy Lou*.

Yellow-white incandescence exploded above them. The biggest hammerhead had tangled with the electrical cable and severed it with one angry snap of its powerful jaws.

They were plunged into darkness.

Bolan tried to gain leverage but the other swimmer hung on with a tenacity fueled by pumping adrenaline. The man shoved Bolan back against the cockpit seat. Bolan gasped as his tank slammed into something hard.

He tried to move, to slide out from under, but his valve tap was snagged fast in an unseen obstacle.

The shifting weight of their struggle had disturbed the fragile balance of the scuttled boat. The hull shuddered as the *Betsy Lou* began to slide from her rocky perch.

Bolan was trapped aboard the vessel as it started to sink into the murky depths beyond the reef. Above him the sharks were threshing in the raging circles of a feeding frenzy.

11

Bolan lay trapped on his back, his breathing apparatus wedged tightly by an obstacle he could not reach. Grogan's man still had hold of his wrist, not daring to let go for an instant in that terrifying darkness.

The *Betsy Lou* lurched forward. Her hull was now grinding against the last of the rocks that restrained it from tumbling into the deeper water.

Bolan's left hand was at the other man's throat, trying to push him off to find room for an emergency maneuver.

He felt a jarring bump as a hungry shark brushed heavily past his extended arm. The fish was abrasively testing his prey. Without the wet suit, Bolan would have had no skin left on his forearm.

Suddenly Bolan saw the man above him jerk violently as a vicious mako carried him off whole in its jaw.

Another tremor ran through the hull. The scuttled wreck teetered on the brink of its final plunge. Even as the swirling undertow seesawed the *Betsy Lou* free from the notch that held her, Bolan slashed through the air tank's retaining straps.

He took one last deep breath and discarded the mouthpiece as the boat slipped away beneath him. The air pockets left trapped within the sunken hull now billowed out in a turbulent rush.

Bolan shot toward the surface, surrounded by this expanding column of huge bubbles. Confused by the seething turbulence, the nearest sharks twisted aside. One old tiger snapped out angrily and tore off Bolan's right flipper.

Through the hissing froth that shielded him, Bolan could make out the dark line of the anchor cable angling down through the surface chop.

Bolan reached out and grabbed the chain. He hauled himself upward hand over hand, not caring that the barnacles lacerated his fingers as he gulped down the first sweet breath of life-giving air.

The currents attempted to twist the *Engracia* from her anchors. The chain Bolan struggled up led to the port side. Grogan's deck team were still rushing around near the starboard railing, trying to figure out what had gone wrong below.

Using his freed right foot and left heel to steady himself, Bolan pulled himself up the ship's side. The inflatable raft was bobbing around at the foot of a wooden ladder amidships.

Against the first faint streaks of dawn, Bolan could see that Judd Cooper was maneuvering the *Ropedancer* dangerously close to the reef. He was less than six hundred yards away and closing.

The crew aboard the *Engracia* were far too busy to see the shadowy bulk of the stealthily approaching vessel, nor did they notice the black-suited figure that slipped onto the deck behind them.

Bolan hid behind the compressor unit to catch his breath. Shots rang out from the starboard side. One of the men was firing wildly with a Colt .45.

"What the hell's happening?" Grogan himself had been dozing on the bridge. He stumbled out of the door above the deck. "What the fuck's going on down there?"

"Sharks!" the winch operator bellowed.

"Shark attack!" the gunman yelled. "Hundreds of 'em."

"Well, don't shoot into the water, you'll hit our..." From his elevated viewpoint, Grogan could make out the darker blotches that stained the water.

The crewmen knew there was little hope for the divers below. A dozen or more fins were cutting back and forth as the sharks searched for any remaining morsel of fresh meat.

Grogan vanished inside to look for his own gun.

Although the men on deck were in no danger themselves, the dreadful fear of those ravenous jaws was infectious. The gunman emptied his Colt, reloaded a fresh clip and blasted away at the ragged dorsal fin of the gargantuan hammerhead.

Bolan tugged off the remaining flipper. He saw a spear gun lying on the deck near some empty air tanks. He knelt on one knee and glanced over the stern. The *Ropedancer* was almost upon them. Cooper could not remain undetected for long. The sky was steadily growing lighter. Bolan realized he had to make his play.

The three crewmen stood at the rail pointing, shouting, watching for any sign that even one of their colleagues had survived the grisly bloodfeast that still churned the waters alongside the salvage ship.

Bolan picked up one of the air tanks and hurled it at the gunman. Before it struck him squarely in the back, the warrior snatched the spear gun and aimed at the next man.

The spear skewered the target's chest as he turned to shout a warning. His call of alarm became a shriek of pain.

The gunner stumbled into the railing. The Colt slipped from his grasp.

Bolan raced down the deck as the third man looked around for a weapon. Lying on the deck beside the pile of cocaine packages they had already recovered was a heavy crowbar. The crewman leaped for this sudden salvation.

Bolan saw a long-handled fire ax mounted to the steel plating. The leather straps had long since rotted in the sea air and salt spray. Bolan ripped it from its moorings.

The crowbar man came in with a two-handed attack. He parried Bolan's first swing with the ax, then stepped forward to hammer down on his opponent. Bolan twisted away and his attacker staggered past.

Bolan unleashed a savage chop at the man's back. The rusted blade severed the base of his spine. Bolan jerked the ax free as the man fell face forward.

From the corner of his eye the Executioner saw that the gunman had regained his breath and dived to recover his Colt.

"Don't even try!" Bolan snarled.

The seaman ignored the warning and made a final lunge for his gun.

The warrior slashed down with the ax, chopping off the man's hand at the wrist. A crimson arc spurted unevenly across the deck as the man screamed his way into merciful oblivion.

"What the...!" Alex Grogan was aghast at the carnage on the deck below him. He stood at the top of the steps holding a Winchester Model 1200 shotgun.

The treasure hunter's mouth dropped open when he saw the *Ropedancer* rapidly pulling alongside. He swung his head back toward the big man who was reaching down to pick up a Colt pistol.

Grogan raised the barrel of the 12-gauge to make target acquisition on the stranger.

Steadying his grip with his left palm, Bolan calmly took aim, allowing for the movement of the deck under his feet. The hammer made only a useless click.... The Colt was empty.

"All right, you bastard!" snarled Grogan. His finger curled back on the trigger.

The steel plate above his head exploded in a sizzling red ball of spitting phosphor flare.

Judd Cooper leaned out of his wheelhouse, the distress pistol still smoking in his hand.

The Winchester boomed, scattering its shot harmlessly skyward as Grogan tumbled down the steps. His T-shirt and hair were aflame.

The flames had splashed along the weathered woodwork of the bridge and now they were being fanned by the early-morning breeze.

Demented by the searing agony, the salvage boss did the first thing that jumped into his pain-scrambled thoughts. He leaped over the railing, seeking relief in the soothing water.

Grogan's body twitched as a hungry predator tugged beneath the waves. His hand appeared once more, then that, too, vanished as the smooth gray hammerhead broke the surface before vanishing into the cobalt depths.

The freshening wind stoked the growing blaze aboard the *Engracia*, also creating a heavy chop. Cooper could not risk bringing the *Ropedancer* any closer for fear of smashing the hull. And there was no way Bolan could cross the shark-infested water to reach him.

"The other side, Skipper!" Bolan shouted. "Pick me up on the port side."

Cooper switched to Reverse, poulling away from the smoking dive ship.

Bolan grabbed one of the cocaine packs and ran across to the far guardrail.

A fuel drum exploded, sending rivulets of hungry fire streaming down the deck. The *Engracia* was turning into a blazing burial ship.

Bolan located the ladder and scrambled down into the inflatable as Cooper rounded the stern.

Three minutes later Bolan tugged himself aboard the *Ropedancer*. Cooper, keeping one eye on the reef, reversed again and drew back from the floating inferno of the *Engracia*.

"I owe you one, Skipper."

"I'll settle for a cigarette," Cooper said, grinning. "Never wanted a smoke or a drink more in my life…and I've run out of both!"

"There's a pack in my shirt pocket," Bolan said, beginning to peel off his wet suit. For the first time he noticed how badly he'd cut his hands. "I'll get them. You take us back to dry land."

Bolan studied the plastic-packed powder in his hand. Now he had the bait that would lure Cardona into making a mistake—the biggest mistake of his whole rancid life.

Drugs had a way of killing people, those who used them and those who trafficked. Someone would soon report the smoke smudge from the dying *Engracia*, but

Bolan and Cooper would be far away before it could be investigated.

This area was the responsibility of the South Florida Task Force, but how long would it be before the GCTF learned of what happened here? And, if Bolan's suspicions were correct, how long after that before Juan Cardona found out that he had lost his drug shipment?

It was around 1:00 P.M. when Cooper tied up alongside the dock at Ward's Yard.

"I'm going to pick up a bottle," he announced, taking a final turn around the bollard. "Mind if I use your car?"

"Go ahead." Bolan did not feel the need for a drink, but he did not begrudge Cooper a shot. Like he'd said, he owed the skipper. Bolan tossed him the keys. "I'll get my stuff together."

Bolan wrapped the cocaine in a brown paper bag. He was stepping up onto the dock as Cooper, whistling to himself, walked through the yard gates.

The sun felt good after the chill, airless depths of that morning's battle.

The concussive effect of the blast knocked Bolan sideways. Reverberating shock waves shattered glass on board the *Ropedancer* as a roiling fireball shot up through the overhanging palm trees.

The car—and Judd Cooper—vanished in one earsplitting roar.

12

"Who are you, really?" Amada Madero asked playfully. Bolan knew he had aroused her curiosity.

His only reply was an enigmatic smile. He would keep his identity secret for a little longer.

The full-length windows leading onto the upper balcony afforded them a panoramic view of the inner bay. The molten disc of the sun was setting in the pass between Sand Key and the southern tip of Clearwater Beach.

Marble statues and a small fountain glowed amid the dark shrubbery in the long garden that sloped right down to the waterfront.

Amada's home was as gracious inside as it was impressive without. She drew the draperies while he lit the candles.

"It's not fair, Mark," she complained. After accepting a glass of wine, Amada confronted him. "You know who I am, don't you?"

Bolan nodded. "I know who you *were*—Maria Ortega."

The slightest tilt of her head acknowledged he was right.

The candlelight caught the highlights in her hair, surrounding her with a delicate halo. Despite her confidence as a businesswoman, at that moment she seemed almost too fragile to have survived the emotional buffeting life had dealt her.

"You may know some of the facts, Mark—although how you found out, I'm not sure—but that is only what happened, not the why of it."

"Tell me," Bolan said.

"I was ambitious," she confessed. "I knew I had talent. But the only way to get ahead is to have powerful friends. That is the same everywhere, it seems. Well, one day I met a police captain..."

"Porcallo."

She shot him a puzzled look before continuing. "Yes, Porcallo. A pig of a man. I was young and impressionable. He made many promises, all were to prove worthless. Later, Porcallo made a gift of me to Castro. To these men, for all their fine words, women are just playthings to·be toyed with, then thrown away. They disgust me."

"There are many ways to get your revenge."

"Sometimes I lie awake at night and dream of that, but it is of no use." Amada took a sip of the wine. "For all my success here in America, I am powerless. Porcallo holds my younger brother Julio prisoner in his headquarters in Santiago del Este."

Bolan made a mental note. Estrada's intelligence network could fill him in on Porcallo's operation out of his Santiago base. Maybe Amada would tell him more.

He would not push her—she seemed far too emotionally tense for that. But at least he now understood why she had refused to provide any assistance to the anti-Communist groups among her fellow exiles.

"When they expelled me, they unwittingly gave me what I had always wanted the most—the freedom to express myself." Her brittle laugh was short and laced with bitterness. "But they kept Julio hostage. He has been in Porcallo's fortress prison for five years.

"Eva Martinez, his girlfriend, is permitted to visit him from time to time. She has remained faithful to Julio. And she is allowed to send me letters occasionally. Eva tells me that he survives from one day to the next. This way they let me know he is still alive. It buys my silence, my passivity."

She slumped forward, resting her head on Bolan's shoulder. He sheltered Amada with his arm as her body shook with long dry sobs of shame and self-recrimination.

Amada had confessed these things to no man other than her protector, Manuel Rivas.

She sat up but looked away, swiping at the tears brimming in her eyes.

"I know you are a man of action," she finally said, seeking to change the subject. "And you say you don't work for the government. So who is the real Mark Bailey?"

"I worked for Washington for a while," Bolan admitted. He still regarded his life as Col. John Phoenix with mixed feelings. "But now I'm a free-lancer again, in more ways than one."

It was obvious he meant something far more dangerous than being a photojournalist.

Bolan put down his glass. "I think I can nail Juan Cardona."

Amada's attitude changed. She faced him squarely, leaning closer.

"I have my own reasons for wanting to trap him." Bolan was not sure if Gouzenkov or the Cuban drug czar had planted the bomb in his car, but Judd Cooper's murder was added to Don Edelman's. There were accounts to be settled. "If you help me corner Cardona, then, when it's done, I'll tell you who I am."

He owed her that much.

Amada sensed this was a blood feud that could only have one outcome.

"Cardona is a cautious man. He has bodyguards at his side everywhere he goes," she warned him.

Bolan knew this. He could have named them. Estrada had picked him up in Bluewater Bay and briefed him well on the way back.

He rose from the couch, picked up the case he had brought with him and deposited the contents on the glass-topped coffee table.

"I want you to make Juan Cardona believe he has finally won you over. You're even to bring him a peace offering...this! It's from a consignment he was expecting, a delivery he has already paid for. Now it's the bait."

A new awareness crossed the woman's features as she began to see the possibilities. "And so as a token of my newfound loyalty, I'm willing to set up the man who is now in possession of it."

"Exactly," Bolan said. "Only Cardona is the one being set up. This isn't talcum powder. He can have his chemical experts test it. It's a shipment of primo cocaine from his Colombian suppliers. Analysis will confirm that this package is from the very same batch that was supposedly lost on a boat called the *Betsy Lou*."

Amada did not ask how he came to be the possessor of this haul. Her concern was for what might happen now. "Cardona will kill you."

"I'd be disappointed if he didn't try," Bolan agreed. "Will you help me set up a meet?"

Bolan radiated a confidence that gave Amada fresh hope. For once, she could feel the odds were tipping against Juan Cardona.

Amada knew she was being used to serve this man's purpose, but it was not in any of the ways she had been used before. This time it was to achieve a mutually satisfying goal.

She could do it.

She would do it.

Amada was the one person who could make Juan Cardona an offer he couldn't refuse—herself.

She would hold out the promise of her body, her being, her love. And she would tempt Cardona with the added sweetness of getting his revenge against the pirate who had ripped him off. It would be too rich a prize for him to resist.

But at this very moment there was a temptation that Amada could not deny herself. She reached out and unbuttoned the top of Bolan's shirt.

"I want you," she murmured. "I need you."

He kissed her forehead as she bent to nuzzle his chest.

Her laughter was playful, carefree at last when she moved back, standing to unzip her dress. Amada let her defenses fall away.

Bolan stood in front of her. Reaching out, he slipped his fingers behind the tantalizing film of her panties, feeling the taut smoothness of her flanks as he pulled Amada against his body.

She tugged at his belt, freeing him to show the strength of his desire. Palms flat against the rigid muscles of his chest, she gently pushed him back onto the couch.

The very tips of her nails raked lightly across his midriff, followed by a trail of warm kisses.

Bolan stroked her shoulders, sending shivers of delight down her spine, then tangled his fingers in her hair as Amada's lips caressed his most sensitive skin.

She forgot the past, the humiliation, the anguish.... Amada was lost in this passionate moment with a man truly worth loving.

13

Juan Cardona smiled and winked at his reflection in the hallway mirror.

He had waited for this moment for a long time—lunch with Amada Madero.

Flushed with this unexpected victory and the heady prospect that soon, very soon, this desirable creature would be his alone, Cardona was doubly delighted with the offering Amada had so thoughtfully brought to placate him.

His men had already reported that a new escort had muscled in on Amada. But for her to be willing to turn this man over to him showed she had the good sense to realize what was best for her in the long run. To settle the score with this thief, Cardona could find it in himself to overlook her former reluctance.

Still, he would be careful.

Cardona fingered one side of his pencil-thin mustache now as he seated himself opposite this vision of loveliness. He briefly let his eyes play on her straining cleavage that was displayed to perfection in the deeply cut pink dress.

There was a twinkle in her eyes as Amada bit slowly into the strawberry dessert. Her tongue snaked across her lip to retrieve a fleck of cream. Cardona could scarcely control his lust for her.

She reached across and took his hand, her fingertips stroking him in feathery circles.

"When he calls the first time, he will want the meeting to take place at midnight."

"Do you know where?"

"Of course," Amada reassured him. "I would not come to you if I did not find out the location."

Cardona refused to think of how she had come by this information. Why should he feel jealous? Soon all this would be in the past. And, as for the man, he would most certainly be dead. But Amada, this...this angel...it almost seemed that betrayal came too easily to her.

"He will call a second time, when you have the money together, and demand that the exchange take place at Chirino's Boat Works. It's on the way to Tarpon Springs."

"I know of it. Just south of Port Joseph."

"Be careful, Juan. This man is dangerous."

Amada looked him straight in the eyes.

Cardona nodded. Oh yes, he intended to take every precaution.

AT THE SUGGESTION of his Cuban ally, Bolan parked his new rental on the far side of a parched softball field. He walked back along the road to the site for his meeting with Cardona.

A row of palm trees, many withered from the freak frost of the previous winter, were silhouetted by the moonlight.

The night warrior checked his watch: 11:25 P.M.

Traffic was light along the distant glowing strip of Alternate Route 19. Cardona should arrive shortly.

The time of the exchange was the only detail Bolan had altered in the scenario discussed with Amada. At the very last moment he had specified that the meet would take place at 11:30 sharp. And he had added a warning: if Cardona missed it, the shipment would be sold to another bidder.

Pedro Estrada had picked the place. Chirino's Boat Works offered a legitimate pull-out service to local yachtsmen and off-season storage for nonresident boat owners. But that was to cover its principal function: the mooring and maintenance of two sleek fishing vessels that served the Cuban's interests.

Estrada knew that sometimes he was closely watched in Miami, so it was useful for him to have boats available to sail at a moment's notice from this quiet harbor on the gulf side.

The main gate led directly into the yard. To the left was Chirino's office and behind it, running across to the water's edge, was the long dark bulk of the main boat-building shed.

On the right of the gate was a retail supply shop and warehouse. A second wooden shed with a tar-paper roof, used mostly for lighter repair work, ran along the northern perimeter of the property.

Between the rear of the repair shop and the dock on that side, standing on a patch of weed-strewn gravel, were a dozen cradles. Half of them carried expensive yachts cocooned under canvas covers. At the end of this row of boats was a back gate where a sandy track led to the main road.

Lamps on the eaves of both sheds crosslighted the large empty yard and cast slivered reflections on the wavelets that lapped at the foot of the launching ramp.

With the water to his back and the buildings forming an uneven semicircle, Bolan judged that except for the main entrance, they were well sheltered from the curious eyes of any late-night drivers going past outside.

He was dressed in jeans, with a dark cotton Windbreaker over a blue T-shirt. The loose fit of the jacket concealed the Jatis, and extra magazines hung from the back of his belt and in elongated thigh pouches. Bolan's seemingly relaxed pose belied his readiness for instant action.

Twin beams illuminated the wire mesh gateway. This time they did not sweep past, but turned in to the boatyard entrance. The gate was open. A Lincoln limousine drove in and braked outside Jose Chirino's office.

The driver killed the lights but left the engine idling.

Bolan remained motionless as a Chevy van wheeled into the yard and stopped in front of the retail store. He would have been surprised if Cardona had not brought his private army with him.

Scarlip was the first to climb out of the big limo. His buddy, the gunsel, appeared from the other side of the car. Their gazes swept over the deserted yard and came to rest on the big man standing alone. Only then did they signal for Cardona to get out.

Just as their boss was making his appearance, nine men clambered out of the van. Led by the unmistakable bulk of Bull Oakum, the soldiers were carrying an assortment of handguns, automatics and two rifles. One of them even clutched an old Thompson.

Bolan recounted the lineup as they positioned themselves behind Cardona.

Three guys were missing already, Bolan noted. They must have been working their way around the back of the retail store, in order to cover him from the repair works to his left.

The two bodyguards flanked Cardona, while Oakum and five of the hired gunslingers spread out in a line from the shop entrance across to the office steps.

"So we meet at last," Cardona said. The dapper Cuban was standing about thirty feet away. He did not have to raise his voice.

"Yeah. But I told you it was to be just me, you and the money," came the ice-cold reply.

"Come now, are you not forgetting something—the shipment?"

"Oh, you'll get what you came for," Bolan promised him. "You've got my word on it."

"Then you must understand why I needed these men. They are here merely to protect the funds. You demanded a large amount of cash, *señor*. And, of course, they are also my insurance that you will hand over the merchandise."

Bolan doubted that Cardona had brought the money. The Cuban must have figured that retrieving the cocaine from one man would be child's play.

The Executioner heard a loose pebble softly chink in the alleyway between the warehouse and the repair shed. On cue, right.

Cardona's artillery was moving into position.

"I would have thought that you too might have brought some companions." Cardona shielded his eyes and scanned the big sheds on either side of the boatyard. "But then perhaps you did."

Bolan's expression gave away nothing.

"It disturbs me to pay twice for what is already rightfully mine," the Cuban complained. A thin film of sweat glistened on his forehead.

Bolan shrugged. "Possession counts for all ten points outside the law, Cardona."

The drug boss was reaching in his pocket for a handkerchief when a smoke grenade struck the gravel halfway between the two men.

Bolan, Jati in hand, rolled away to one side as a hail of bullets chewed up the ground where he had been standing.

Estrada was not going to wait and see if Cardona's movement was the signal—*el espectro*'s life depended on his instant judgment.

From their rooftop vantage point Rafael Santos and his brother, Roberto, used their MM-1s to lay down a second round of hissing, billowing confusion. Estrada simultaneously killed the lights.

A solid stack of railroad ties offered Bolan the perfect cover for return fire.

Cardona had vanished, quickly retreating behind the smoke cloud. A twisted skein of wraiths was tugged aside by the invisible hand of a midnight breeze to reveal the shadowy figure of Scarlip still seeking a target.

Bolan took one-handed aim and unleashed the wicked Finnish SMG. The first burst caught Scarlip in the chest. The second one smeared the scowl on his face into a death mask.

Weaving around to the other side of the ties, Bolan used his second weapon to sweep the space at the back of the warehouse. A startled yelp of pain marked a hit.

Roberto Santos lobbed a grenade at the limousine. The explosive landed in front of the grille and bounced underneath. The Lincoln erupted in a double flash as the grenade ignited the fuel system. The driver perished as the car disintegrated in a fiery thunderball. Scarlip's buddy was knocked flat, shredded with shrapnel.

"Kill them!" Cardona ordered in a hoarse shriek as he staggered toward the protection of the shop. "Kill them all!"

Chirino and his foreman, Miguel Alonso, were concealed behind the repair building. Both were holding Ingrams from Estrada's arsenal. As Cardona's men attempted to flee over the perimeter fence at the back, the two shipbuilders made their hidden presence felt. The would-be escapers found themselves trapped in converging lanes of fire.

One man, his fingers hooked into the chain link, stood there shuddering spasmodically with each successive impact as a full magazine tore into him. The other two did not even make it to the fence.

"More smoke!" Bolan called out.

Rafael Santos responded with a fresh grenade targeted perfectly on the far side of the launch ramp.

Bolan made a dash for the nearest of the boat cradles.

Estrada, nursing a Savage 69-N, had slipped down from the rooftop and scanned the yard. He saw Cardona crouching behind the moonfaced thug with the Tommy gun. They were clearly lit by the flames of the crackling wreckage.

At Cardona's instructions the gunman sprayed the yard wildly while his boss used this distraction to scamper away behind the store.

The dull booming roar of Estrada's Savage answered the harsh chatter of the submachine gun. The first load blew in the front end of the van. The second clipped the gunner; steel pellets at the expanding edge of the spread scoured his scalp down to the bone.

Screaming, he rushed blindly toward the shop front. Estrada pumped in another shell. This round shattered the supply-store window and draped the rag-doll body of the hardman over the jagged teeth of broken glass.

Bolan was still crouching by the keel of a Wavecrest thirty-four-footer. Through the veils of acrid gunsmoke he could see that the exploding car had set light to the front of the office. And he could hear Estrada clearing up the yard in a decidedly final fashion.

The Executioner's position gave him an unobstructed line of sight down the front of the workshop and into the gap behind the warehouse. He saw Cardona trying to weasel behind the cover of a packing crate.

The nighthitter rose to one knee, a gun in each hand, and poured twin streams of hollowpoint retribution at Cardona's hiding place. The Cuban staggered back into the open.

"This is for Don," Bolan muttered. "And this is for Judd Cooper."

Squeezing both triggers for a complete pull, Bolan discharged a 9mm barrage that spun Cardona on a skittering pirouette into hell.

A shot came from the roof. The Ingram popped once more behind the repair shop. There could not be many left.

Bolan snapped home a fresh magazine and was reaching for another when a brawny forearm locked like a vise around his throat. Bolan dropped the guns and grabbed the hand that was circling in for his heart.

Bull Oakum!

Bolan managed to twist the blade away from his chest as the two men shuffled backward. Oakum was too heavy to shrug off. Bracing his legs, Bolan pumped upward with all his might.

He lifted the giant clear in the air, driving the top of his polished skull into the Wavecrest's propeller blade. Once...twice... He heaved Oakum on his back, hammering that gleaming dome against the bronze edge of the prop.

Oakum's grip loosened and Bolan jerked free. He executed a forward roll and snatched up the nearest of the discarded Jatis.

The muscle-bound psychopath stood with one hand clamped over the streaming gashes in his cranium, the other lifting back to throw the knife.

Bolan fired from the prone position. He stitched short bursts right up Oakum's body.

The brute wobbled to the edge of the launching ramp—more dead on his feet than alive—and hesitated, as if he wondered how warm the water was before crashing over onto the sloping concrete.

Bull Oakum lay there like a beached whale in the moonlight, the greasy waves lapping over his trouser legs.

Cars were screeching to a halt outside the gates. Spotlights were played in a dazzling zone around the entrance and a loudspeaker began blaring instructions.

"Drop your weapons!"

14

"You are surrounded by the police." Despite the tinny amplification Bolan recognized Leo Webber's voice. "Come out with your hands up!"

The night warrior checked the time: it was ten minutes before midnight. He judged there were four, maybe five, cars out there on the road. It was doubtful that Webber had enough men to completely surround the perimeter fence of Chirino's yard, but this was no time to call the investigator's bluff.

Estrada, followed by the Santos brothers, emerged from the smoke-tinged darkness. He gave a low whistle. "Jose...Miguel...over here!"

They were soon assembled on the seawall at the farthest point from the gates.

"Time for us to leave, *amigo*." Estrada gestured to Bolan that they were going over the edge. In the distance a Coast Guard patrol boat with its spotlights already sweeping the surface was approaching fast.

Chirino went first, then the other men. Estrada tugged Bolan's sleeve. "You follow them. I'll bring up the rear."

Bolan lowered himself over the wall. The tide was on the turn, the water was about three feet deep and the bottom muddy.

To Bolan's right Chirino had levered open the grating that covered a storm-sewer outlet. It was obvious they had used this escape route before. Holding his weapons well clear of the water, Bolan waded toward the drain.

"Rafael knows the way," the Cuban rebel whispered as Bolan ducked behind the metal bars. Ahead of him a dim circle of light glowed deep within the musty tunnel. Stooping, he paddled after the others.

The big pipe was slippery with weed growth and decaying debris. It led the men back under the road, turned south and emerged in a concrete culvert that ran along the edge of the softball park. A fringe of bushes covered them from the commotion outside Chirino's Boat Works.

"I'll be home in bed before the police arrive to tell me what's happened," said Chirino, then he slipped away under the dark trees.

"Another gang war between rival groups of Cuban expatriates. It is suspected that drugs may be involved." Estrada mimicked the news stories that were bound to appear. He turned to Bolan. "I'll stay with Rafael tonight. Roberto has a place prepared for—"

"No. I have other business to attend to first."

"If you need more firepower, I have the guns," Estrada reminded him. "If you need my men, they are yours to command. And if you need a fast boat, Ramon Morales has moved the *Alicia* down the coast. It is fueled and ready."

"No, this is something I must take care of alone."

In the distance they could hear Webber shouting orders for his men to close in.

"If you had not changed the time of the meeting at the last moment, the cops and the DEA boys would have been in place to scoop us all up."

"Yeah," Bolan growled. "It's as if Cardona called them in for protection."

But another suspicion niggled at Bolan, one he did not want to give voice to. It pained him to think that Amada Madero might have double-crossed them all.

BOLAN DROVE SOUTH on Bayshore Boulevard, over the railroad tracks and through sleepy Dunedin.

He wondered how far the cocaine traffic had spread its vicious poison. Its organization was not a monolithic structure like a modern army or a slick business corporation, despite the media's popular image, but a pervasive network of corruption that tainted everyone it touched.

The Mafia, the Colombian families, the renegade Cubans and a host of bankers, attorneys and ambitious hoodlums formed a kinship of evil that profited from their countless victims' broken health and ruined careers, shattered families and abandoned dreams.

They were a loose-knit federation built on greed and illicit gratification, fear and favors, bribery and beatings, and police and political payoffs.

Estrada's inquiries had indicated the extent, but no specific names, of Juan Cardona's connections with the very establishment pledged to serve and enforce the law.

Cardona himself had never been successfully prosecuted. There were always sufficient funds to pay for fancy lawyers and to meet the bail for any close associates, which they then skipped out on.

Any evidence that was amassed would mysteriously vanish. And time after time Cardona's rivals would be harassed and hit hard by raids and arrests while he continued to prosper.

Well, all that had ended tonight. Cardona had come face-to-face with the one man all his rotten wealth could never have bought. The Executioner would not look the other way when it came to a callous conspiracy that thrived on the misery of others.

The way Bolan figured it now, he had been fingered from the moment he introduced himself to Sheriff Buford Johnson back on that bridge over Marriot's Swamp. And he could not help but suspect that even Peter Ziman might have been involved, too.

Suppose the well-dressed agent was a user and more than likely in over his head. It would have been easy enough to twist the arm of an addict in that situation. It would certainly explain why Webber had been so keen to personally supervise his tour of the GCTF facilities—it was almost as if Bolan had been expected.

Guys like Johnson and Ziman had no idea who were the powers they served. A couple of phone calls followed by an envelope stuffed with bills or a package of those magic white crystals took care of small-timers like them.

Loyalty was cheap that low down on the heap. To bosses like Cardona, they were merely hired help who could be bought or sold without making a dent in the petty cash.

Men like Leo Webber exacted a higher toll, but the enormous profits of a growing drug empire could meet any price they named.

Bolan wondered about tonight's operation. And again the nagging suspicion that Amada had been willing to sacrifice him to make sure that Cardona would never trouble her again, continued to plague him. The temptation of revenge for Manuel Rivas might have been stronger than the love she professed for him. Bolan knew how that could eat into the soul.

He parked under the avenue of ancient trees, draped with the silver-gray beards of Spanish moss, that lined the quiet street outside Amada's mansion.

She was waiting for him in the main lounge. A single candle was lit; a single glass of wine had been poured.

"I...I thought you would call." She kissed him on the cheek.

"You're celebrating already? You must have been confident of the outcome."

"Yes, because I believe in you." She poured a second drink. "Tell me what happened."

He gave her an abbreviated account of the evening's activities.

"These men who arrived, they were working for Cardona?"

"That's one possibility," Bolan conceded.

"Then it was as he said."

"What's that?"

"I was present when Cardona first proposed that he and Manuel expand into the drug business. It happened right here in this room. I remember three things...besides Manuel's adamant refusal, that is. Cardona said he had a contact, someone very well placed, who could neutralize the impact of the American authorities in this area."

"Like the assistant director of investigations for the Gulf Coast Task Force."

She nodded. "This Leo Webber you spoke of...and Cardona also claimed that he could finance much of the operation himself. Later, when we were alone, Manuel wondered how Cardona could come up with the kind of capital it required."

"A sleeping partner?"

"Yes, that was the third thing. But Cardona also mentioned that this other backer was the same man who could ensure that the boats would get past all defense systems and drop off their cargoes at safe landing points. Cardona was excited. He told Manuel it was foolproof. No one would ever suspect how it worked. He was enraged when Manuel turned him down flat."

Bolan had a pretty clear idea of the silent partner's identity, but he was far from silent, in fact he was saturating the gulf region with his broadcasts twenty-four hours a day.

Leo Webber had introduced Juan Cardona to his father-in-law, Magnus Angell. They were the unholy triumvirate who had gone into business with Castro's wholesale operation.

One question remained unanswered.

"Why did he need Manuel at all?" Bolan asked.

"Manuel Rivas was a powerful patron, a man with many influential contacts. But he was an implacable enemy if you abused his trust. As long as Manuel was alive, Cardona would never have dared start up an independent operation in this region."

The same way that the Sicilians would have carved up a territory and controlled it, Bolan thought.

"You know where the drug came from, don't you?"

"*Sí*, I have a good idea," Amada admitted. "From Cuba, no? I think Carlos Porcallo was involved."

She dried up, trying to think through where all this was leading.

Bolan realized that Amada probably knew very little about the inner workings of the Cuban connection, far less than Estrada's intelligence feelers would be able to uncover for him. They would have been much more careful than that. And now he also wondered why he had ever doubted her sincerity.

"You're going there, aren't you? To Cuba. You're going to try to stop them. That's what all this is about."

Amada touched his sleeve. The concern, the fear in her eyes was very real. She did not want to lose him.

Bolan did not answer, but inside he knew she was right. The trail led back to Porcallo and Santiago del Este. What did Jacques Terrence say in Paris? No one dare strike against Castro's island fortress for fear of touching off a war; that was the immunity the drug smugglers counted on.

Well, it already was a war. Leo Webber had admitted that much, even if he lied about which side he was on. The drug traffickers were the ones who had declared it.

It was time for the Executioner to strike back with a lightning raid that would teach those scum that nowhere in the world was beyond the reach of justice.

"I wish I could help you. No, I wish I could stop you. Honestly, if I had any information I would gladly give it to you, but I know very little of what went on in Porcallo's headquarters." Amada walked toward the open window. A storm was flickering through the clouds to the southwest. "These men care for nothing except their own power and prestige. They'll keep Julio imprisoned for life if it makes them feel just a little safer."

Bolan moved behind her and gently clasped Amada around the waist. She half turned toward him. "Let's go out on the balcony. I want to watch the storm."

He let her go. She looked up at the racing clouds as the first fat drops of warm rain splattered down. Her mouth curved in a mischievous grin, then she beckoned him.

Bolan stepped outside, too.

"Have you ever made love in a thunderstorm?"

Amada Madero felt a strange tranquillity. The man she loathed was no more and Rivas was revenged. After they had made love in that special glow of togetherness she would find out who Mark Bailey really was. There was so much for them to share.

Eyes flashing and lips moist with expectation, she turned, spinning him around in the fierce rush of her embrace.

Suddenly her smile of triumph was obliterated by the sudden shock of pain.

Amada's head snapped back and she gave one gasping cough.

The soft phutt that followed and Bolan's snarl of rage were both smothered by the rumbling peal of thunder. Even as he set her down, still cradled in his arms, he saw the pale flash of a figure racing down the garden steps.

"Amada..."

"Ssh, let me talk...not much time...one thing I must ask..."

Bolan's hands were sticky with the hot flow of blood. How could he explain everything to her now? The obscene stain was spreading so fast. Amada had only a few moments left.

"Promise me..." her voice dropped to a painful, husky whisper. "Mark, promise me one thing. Get Julio out of their clutches...rescue my brother...."

Bolan nodded. Her eyes fluttered closed. Amada's face was at peace.

"Yes, I will." She would not hear him, but it was a blood oath he was sworn to keep.

Bolan carried her to the couch, kissed her and ran from the room. Leaping down the stairs, he raced for his car.

The Executioner's thoughts were racing, too. The killer would not have dared to leave his getaway transport parked right outside. He would probably have to cover two or three blocks to reach it, and he only had a minute, maybe eighty seconds head start at the most.

The side street was a dead-end road leading down to a fishing pavilion. Bolan turned the other way, scanning left and right. He saw no one from the first intersection.

He accelerated for another block. Looking right, he glimpsed a figure running flat out for a parked car. Bolan wrenched the wheel and gunned the engine. The rear of the Buick fishtailed as it pulled out ahead of him.

The Executioner had no doubt who the assassin was.

This time Gouzenkov ignored the rules of the road. The streets were quiet at this late hour. He ran straight through a red to increase his lead.

Bolan followed hard on his heels.

The intermittent showers had left the road surface slippery. Both cars slithered at high speed around the curve alongside the golf course. Bolan came up fast on the outside, pushing ninety-five as he drew abreast of the Buick.

Trees, thick shrubbery and a fence lined the shoulder to the right. No civilians, a clear field of fire. Bolan nudged the wheel and slammed into the side of the other car.

Gouzenkov wrestled to keep control. Bolan rammed him again in an explosion of torn chrome and grinding metal.

The Russian killer braked, trying to force his pursuer to overshoot. But Gouzenkov had not allowed for the rain-slicked surface. The tail end swung around, he tried to correct, then the Buick spun as it jumped onto the grass shoulder.

Bolan was slowing just as the assassin's car crashed sideways into the metal fence.

Both men emerged at the same moment. Gouzenkov, too shaken to have retrieved his P36 from the car, took one look at the American, vaulted onto the roof of the wrecked Buick, jumped over the fence and vanished into the bushes.

Bolan was nearly two hundred yards down the road. The Jati was in his hand. He marked the spot where Gouzenkov had disappeared, then he too ran toward the fence.

A long sign was wired in place about twenty feet to Bolan's right.

Welcome to JungleLand.
Wild Animals in Their Natural Habitat.

Right.

Petr Gouzenkov had gone to earth in the very terrain that had forged the Executioner.

15

Bolan crouched in the darkness, pausing to let his vision adjust to the gloomy undergrowth. The storm was becoming a distant barrage as it moved out to sea. The rain it had spilled dripped from the leaves and branches to be soaked up by the humus underfoot.

Mack Bolan was back in the jungle, the hellzone he knew so well, the battleground he had never really left.

The designers of this zoological showplace had done their work well. In the middle of the Suncoast tourist playground they had recreated the quintessential environment of the humid tropics, where nature still roamed red in tooth and claw. It was a savage, deadly world to which the Executioner was especially attuned.

His senses on the alert, the soldier breathed in the familiar smells of damp earth and rotting vegetation. Sector by sector he scanned the mottled byplay of the shadows swaying and shifting as the last of the thunderclouds raced past the moon.

The rustling, whirring chorus of myriad insects was punctuated by curious snuffles and vigilant sniffing as larger animals stirred restlessly, sensing the alien intruders.

Somewhere to his right Bolan heard a twig snap. It was too heavy and too careless to be anything other than a man.

The night hunter eased forward through the bushes. He opened the plastic handgrip and charged the Jati, still listening and watching for the stealthiest movement that would mark his opponent. Slowly he began to circle the back of the flamingo pond.

The quarry broke cover. Bolan heard his muffled steps racing down an asphalt path that led deeper into the complex maze of JungleLand. Was he fleeing in a desperate attempt to save his own skin? Or trying to lure his American target into a more favorable position for an ambush?

Bolan reached the end of the small lake and followed him, gliding softly through the greenery parallel to the public walkway. The fetid odor of the nearby alligator swamp warned him to veer closer to the path.

This was the arena in which the fighting skills of Sergeant Mercy had been honed to lethal perfection.

Everything connected.

This moment was linked to his own past in the killing ground of Vietnam, and to all the other brave men who had struggled, fought and learned to survive in the jungles of the world.

It was a unique battlefield in which the terrain itself was every bit as hostile as the enemy. It was a malignant world far removed from parade grounds and peace conferences.

The jungle never begged for a truce.

Here the soldier practiced caution and sharpened his skills, or he did not survive.

Here the fighter learned to endure from footstep to danger-filled footstep.

From breath to breath.

From heartbeat to heartbeat.

He learned to live and die alone.

And so from Nam to now, and until he took that last long plunge into the unknown beyond, Bolan was and always would be the existential warrior.

He had left the struggle for Southeast Asia only to find there was no escape from his destiny. Packs of human vermin were turning his homeland into a stinking jungle of murder, corruption, filth and violence.

His own family had been devoured. Bolan's private war, this ongoing campaign, had started as a personal vendetta before it became a broader crusade.

He had long ago decided that individual hatred had no place in his mission.

He did not fool himself into thinking that one bright morning he would wake victorious, the last enemy of decency and order vanquished, and he could at last lay down his arms. Human nature ensured the battle would continue. Each man must make a choice. It did not take a fancy education and intellectual double-talk to tell the difference between right and wrong.

The bosses in the Kremlin, their underlings like Strakhov and puppets like Fidel Castro had chosen power at the expense of those ill-equipped to resist them. Men like Cardona, Webber and Magnus Angell had chosen to profit from the weakness of others.

And warrior Bolan had made *his* commitment. It was an honorable choice. He could live with it and, when the time came as come it must, he would die at peace with himself.

This was just one more round in the never-ending conflict. Gouzenkov had pledged his talents to the service of evil. Bolan was sworn to oppose him and all his kind. Here they would clash once more.

Drawing on grim experience—and perhaps calling upon a shared pool of collective wisdom from warriors past—Bolan sifted through the abundance of sensory input, focusing only on those sights, sounds and smells that warned of impending danger or drew him closer to the elusive quarry.

The bushes thinned out ahead, opening onto a broad sloping plain. The huge bulk of an elephant rested in a sand pit about thirty feet away. The big bull raised a wary head. Bolan silently backtracked to the path.

A peacock strutted by, tail feathers still ruffled, disturbed by the passing of an unauthorized visitor. Gouzenkov must be ahead of him.

They were now at least half a mile from the main road; no unnatural sounds penetrated this far through the luxuriant tangle of the JungleLand thickets.

The path forked. One branch curved out of sight around the wall of the sunken hippo pen, the other led across a wooden bridge over the stream that fed the bird ponds.

Two or three tiny clumps of mud indicated that the Russian killer had crossed the bridge. Anyone who knew his way around here would have stuck to the paved paths. It was a thirty-foot gap with no possibility of cover. Bolan paused to take stock.

Suddenly he tensed, tucking in tighter behind a concrete wastebin, the Jati raised and ready. He had detected the faintest squeak of a shoe on the trail behind him.

Bolan waited, scarcely breathing, as the footsteps drew closer.

If the other man had not started whistling to himself he would have been playing a harp. Two bars of "Yellow Submarine" were all that saved him from the harsher music of the Jati.

A night watchman, bundled under a plastic rain cape, sauntered past.

Bolan relaxed fractionally. His reflexes had been on a hair trigger.

The guard stopped by the hippopotamus enclosure, fumbled under his poncho for a flashlight, and played the beam down on the occupants. Then he flicked off the light and strolled down the fork toward the refreshment area.

Bolan went the other way, past the hippo pen, stooping low as he hastened for the dark overhang of the trees beyond.

He could smell big cats near at hand...and he sensed danger.

Gouzenkov was close, very close.

A tall bird-and-animal food dispenser blocked the shoulder ahead of Bolan, partially obscuring his view. He crept closer to the machine, still shielded by the shadow-giving trees above, trying to get a fix on the enemy. He crouched on one knee, the tilted muzzle of the Jati slowly traversing the path.

The Executioner knew that Gouzenkov was no stranger to this kind of terrain. And Bolan was certain that the Spetsnaz officer knew every trick in the manuals of the Red Army, the GRU and the KGB.

Bolan studied the bushes on the far side of the path. He could still feel that warning tingle, then intuition and reflex fused into action. Bolan rolled sideways from the kneeling position just as Gouzenkov dropped from the branch above him.

The two men sprawled on the grass, each grappling for the advantage. The brawny Russian grabbed Bolan's gun arm and repeatedly smashed the back of his hand against the edge of the asphalt paving. The SMG was jarred loose.

Gouzenkov made a sudden grab for the Jati. Bolan wrestled him away, bringing his knee up hard between the killer's legs.

Teeth clenched with pain, the assassin gripped Bolan's upper body and swung him across the path. Both men banged hard into the retaining wall on the other side.

The American staggered to his feet. They were both breathing harshly now, but Gouzenkov jackknifed upward, ramming his head into Bolan's gut. Seizing the advantage, the Russian wrapped him in a bear hug and forced him back.

The wall was four feet high with a rough, flat top. Using his full weight, Strakhov's ace bent Bolan's spine back over the concrete. Pain lanced outward from the unhealed bruise. Bolan knew he could not keep his footing much longer against such relentless pressure.

Gouzenkov laced his fingers under his opponent's chin and began to lever him completely off-balance.

Bolan threw out one hand and grasped the wall, testing his grip. His legs came up in a scissor movement, which pulled Gouzenkov on top of him, and with one heave, both men flipped over the edge.

The Russian murderer made a frantic grab for Bolan's jacket, missed and tumbled headlong into the pit.

The Executioner was left dangling by one arm. His other hand snaked up and grasped the top of the wall. Finding hidden reserves of energy, fueled with the adrenaline of self-preservation, Bolan pulled himself to safety.

The hungry roar of JungleLand's prized black panther echoed through the park as slashing claws and razor sharp fangs tore into the hapless Russian sniper.

A second great cat, determined not to be cheated of its share, sprang forward with a bloodcurdling snarl. They played with Gouzenkov, tugging him this way and that as they ripped him apart for their feast.

16

The *Alicia* headed south-southeast. Feathery trails of cirrus were fleeting wisps against the spangled backdrop of the velvet night sky. The lights of a large tanker lay far off the starboard beam.

Ramon Morales eased the craft up to three-quarters speed and the big 892 diesel responded with a comfortable growl.

Estrada, the Santos brothers and Morales—they were the true revolutionaries. Bolan was still a youth when these men, then hardly more than boys themselves, were fighting in the Sierra Maestra.

They had wanted to play their part in sweeping away the despotic regime of Batista. They had earnestly discussed land reform, but with honestly scheduled repayments for those estates affected. And, knowing how their island's economy was tied to the export of sugar, they wanted to retain America as a friend, ally and trading partner.

They wanted a new Cuba.

But they needed a leader who could unite the rival factions and galvanize the Cuban people into decisive action.

They got a charismatic chief, all right, Fidel Castro.

But they lost their beloved island.

After loudly proclaiming to all the world that he could never be a Marxist, Castro embraced the thugs in the Kremlin. He swallowed their ideology hook, line and sinker, spewing back up the propaganda in seven-hour harangues to the deluded crowds of Havana.

He had encouraged his countrymen to fight for independence, then sold them out to Moscow. Now, "that greaseball," as Morales called him, could not survive without Soviet arms, advisers and aid, which he willingly paid for with young Cuban blood spilled in distant battle zones on behalf of his Russian masters.

The atmosphere aboard the *Alicia* was taut with barely subdued excitement. Each man tried to contain his feelings now that they were returning, albeit briefly, to the island they loved so well. But *el espectro* would be the only one going ashore with the American fighter to raid Porcallo's headquarters.

Bolan had not asked him to volunteer—it would have been pointless—and, for his part, Estrada was already committed to going all the way as Bolan's flanker.

After a short telephone conference with the leading Cuban, requesting that the *Alicia* and its crew be ready to leave that evening, Bolan had rested up for the day. He knew the final round would be the most grueling.

A "surprised" Chirino was still helping the local police with their inquiries, despite Webber's insistence that the boatbuilder was somehow involved in the midnight massacre. But Jose Chirino claimed he was an honest man and had the books to prove it. Luckily, he also had the insurance to cover the damages that so "outraged" him.

Roberto Santos was watching the ghostly orange sweep of the radar, waiting to spell Ramon at the wheel. His brother Rafael was aft, inspecting the fishing gear that would cover their real purpose in sailing these waters.

Estrada checked that all was proceeding quietly according to plan, then smoothed out a chart on the cabin table.

"Mack, this is where we are...and here's where we're going." Estrada's finger traced a course past the Dogleg Bank, through the deep soundings of the Santaren Channel, then farther south following the Old Bahama, to where the cays and islands of Camagüey lay like broken vertebrae chipped off the tortured spine of Cuba's north-central coastline. "Here, sheltered behind the reefs of Cayo Vincente, lies the little port of Santiago del Este."

"It's certainly well hidden."

"The inlet at Santiago is a natural harbor. In the old days it was used by pirates. The Spaniards wiped them out and built a fort there to make sure the buccaneers would never return.

"Over the years the fortress fell into disuse. Then the villagers used it as a storehouse. Soldiers came again and for a while it was an armory. For many years, until the arrival of Carlos Porcallo, it was the harbor master's office."

"The town isn't too big?"

"More like an overgrown village. Mostly fishermen and dockhands for the small interisland traders who call here. It's also home for some of the sugarcane workers." Estrada ran his fingertip in a semicircle around Santiago's hinterland. "Agricultural, and nearly all in sugar production. A quiet and backward region from which the tourists are kept away."

"How long has Porcallo been stationed there?"

"For seven long years. Hating every moment of it almost as much as the townspeople loathe him. But Porcallo knows he is serving his boss well. Even his rank has been kept artificially low so as not to attract attention to his real work. He'll wait to enjoy his rewards. Castro could not have picked a more dedicated man to set up his drug pipeline."

"How do they work it?"

"The drugs, mostly from Colombia, are landed on the southern coast and quickly trucked to Santiago. There is a storage vault at Porcallo's headquarters. When they are ready to make a run, a fast patrol boat takes the load through the reefs to a waiting mother ship.

"They make the transfer under cover of darkness. Then this mother ship, looking like an innocent freighter, cruises northward as far as the Cay Sal Bank where the drugs are again transferred, this time to the waiting smugglers."

"So the double transfer ensures that no direct contact is ever observed between the Cuban authorities and the American drug runners."

"*Sí*, this way they can claim their hands are clean of any involvement."

It still did not answer how the blockade runners knew when and where it was safest to make their trips to the Florida coast.

"Any more details on the headquarters?"

"Of course, *amigo*. You asked for the fullest intelligence possible. There were many real criminals kicked out with political refugees via Mariel. I myself have talked with a man confined in Santiago before being transferred to La Cabana. And another man from Combinada del Este had a cell mate who had been imprisoned by Captain Porcallo. There is also this," Estrada said. He produced a sheet of paper. "Using the information from the ex-convicts, I have made this diagram for you."

The inlet was shaped like a slightly squashed and irregular keyhole. The fort sat squarely on the stubby point of land protruding on the right of the harbor entrance.

Around its entire perimeter ran a stout seawall. The outer stones faced the surf pounding across the reefs that were Santiago's natural defense. In contrast, the leeward side offered a deep, sheltered inlet.

Estrada had drawn in the outline of a boat tied to this stone wharf immediately behind the fortress.

"Is this where they keep the patrol boat?"

"*Sí.* Russian built. Very fast. With twin fifties."

Bolan nodded. He was familiar with the type.

"It is moored opposite the main entrance. The crew is billeted with the rest of Porcallo's men, a small handpicked unit of militia detached to serve on special duty."

Estrada pointed to the two wooden barracks he had sketched inside the courtyard.

The fort itself was a hexagon of massive rock walls built to withstand the bombardment of heavy cannons. Each of the six corners was a tower slightly taller than the connecting walls; only narrow windows and gun slits faced the outside. It was austere, impregnable and perfect for its purpose.

The inner compound now contained the two barracks, a garage for military transport, a storage shed and a wired-off enclosure against the northeast wall.

"What's this dotted line?"

"Porcallo had a section of the inner yard fenced off as an exercise pen for his prisoners. When they are allowed visitors, this is where the meetings take place, in full view of both the guards in the yard and those on the walls above.''

"And the prisoners are kept wnere...? In this tower?''

"That's right. The dungeons are carved out of solid rock.''

"How many men is he holding at any one time?''

"Not too many. Six, maybe eight. Usually they are men who have crossed Porcallo, personally or politically,'' Estrada told Bolan. "After a rigged trial in Camagüey they are transferred to serve their time in prisons like Melna-2 or La Cabana.''

"Did you find out anything on Julio Ortega?''

Bolan had not forgotten his promise.

"The men I talked to seemed to think that there were two prisoners kept permanently in Santiago. They are segregated from the rest. One is a local youth—he might well be this Julio Ortega you speak of—the other is an American, Paul Lewis Canfield.''

"The financier's son? Thought he vanished at sea?''

"Apparently he got mixed up in a smuggling venture, a drug deal that went sour, and now he is Porcallo's guest in the fort at Santiago.''

"What was all the noise Jesse Jackson made in the primaries? Didn't he bring back the Americans Castro had imprisoned?''

El espectro snorted in derision.

"They only let Jackson have the ones it suited them to be rid of,'' said Estrada.

Bolan was not interested in political grandstanding. His attention returned to the drawing. It would be suicide to try to storm the place from the sea, but the landward approach offered little better prospects.

"How far in can you take the *Alicia*?"

"Depends on the weather and naval activity in the area. Not much closer than six or seven miles. After that you and I will take the whaler. We'll land here in this cove." Estrada indicated a tiny nick in the shoreline about eight miles to the east of Santiago. "Felix Vargas will meet us there. He was radioed last night from Miami. Vargas was one of the men sent ashore in the Mariel Harbor mix-up. Been working as a fisherman in this region."

"And what's his real purpose?"

"Oh, a little sabotage now and then," the Cuban said, grinning. "But mostly he's sounding out all those who can be counted on to resist the regime when the time for a showdown comes. Many are sympathetic, some will actively help us. Porcallo himself is our best recruiter!"

"Why do they call him *el loco*?"

"Because he has the meanest, craziest temper and the power to use it. I will tell you a story, *amigo*. When I was a kid I played ball with a buddy named Esteban Aguero. My friend had magic hands. Esteban was going to be a major league star. Now, Esteban's old man didn't like Batista, but after the revolution he wasn't going to kiss Castro's ass, either. Carlos Porcallo was then setting up the DGI. He tried to get Esteban to betray his own father, but my friend wouldn't do it. Porcallo lost his temper and crushed Esteban's fingers."

Estrada paused to light up. It still made him angry to remember what happened to his friend.

"What about the Russians?"

"They're all over the place. They have a rest area, a private beach, just outside Santiago. My people regard them as pigs. Vargas should have more information on the latest Soviet movements in this region.''

"Any Russians in the fort?''

"Not that I know of. At least, not stationed there.''

"And this spit of land the fort is on is completely fenced off.'' Bolan ran his finger along the line Estrada had marked.

The Cuban nodded. "From the oceanfront to the inner harbor. Permanently lit up. The nearest buildings are these fishermen's sheds down here. The town itself is at the bottom end of the inlet and around the opposite shore. It will be very difficult to approach Porcallo's headquarters.''

The cabin grew thick with smoke as they studied the sketch. Bolan and the tough freedom fighter drank cups of syrupy Cuban coffee as they considered every option.

"Cayo Vincente ahead,'' called out Morales, who had taken back the wheel. He knew these waters well and would guide the *Alicia* in as close as he dared.

The landing team got dressed as the Santos brothers readied the whaler. The outboard was heavily muffled for more or less "silent'' running.

They donned dark utility clothes. Estrada wore a baseball cap with no badge; Bolan put on a thin woolen watch cap. They carried machetes and canteens on their belts, and each had a compass and compact survival kit. Their weapons had been well oiled against the elements.

Rafael was stowing a backpack full of spare ammo and explosives. Roberto carried out the small transceiver with RDF to home in on the *Alicia* for the pickup. Morales slowed for them to maneuver the boat securely alongside.

They welcomed the fresh night air after the staleness of the cabin. Estrada clambered down into the smaller boat. Bolan made a final check and moved to the rail.

"*Caramba!* Patrol approaching!"

Morales had spotted the glowing blip on the edge of the Raytheon screen. He touched the finger pad for an 8-mile display, reduced the clutter from the waves along the shallows of the nearby reef and adjusted the gain control. There was no mistaking it.

"Navy patrol. Six miles off at most and closing fast!"

17

All illumination aboard the *Alicia* had been doused. She was cruising parallel to the cay's undersea shelf at less than four knots.

The running lights of the patrol vessel could be seen as colored pinpricks off the starboard quarter.

"Look!" Roberto pointed ahead.

The horizon in front of them was blotted out by a thick mantle of predawn fog.

"Rápido," Ramon shouted from the wheelhouse. "Get the boat away and we'll both make it."

There was no time for well-wishing.

Bolan swung over into their landing launch. Estrada had the engine started. Phosphorescent particles sparkled in its wake as the whaler ran for the uncertain protection of the reef.

The dark bulk of the *Alicia* raced toward the mist, a mere shadow on the sea as it purposely decoyed the gunboat farther south.

"We'll have to trust that we're lost in the sea clutter on their radar," Bolan said, checking their compass heading.

The modified V hull skipped nimbly through the tricky shallows. Estrada's skin was beaded with salt spray as he glanced back.

"It's working. They're following the *Alicia*. Huh, they won't catch Ramon before he's well clear of the territorial limit."

The silhouette of the Komar-class coastal patrol craft passed well astern of them. It was speeding after the intruding fishing vessel.

Bolan watched the waters to his left. The South Vincente beacon was falling behind them; they were in the calmer seas of the lagoon behind the reef. He scanned the black band of the shoreline watching for the signal from Felix Vargas.

Five minutes passed. "Over there! A little to our right. Flashing in groups of three."

"That's the sign," said Estrada, quietly praying that it was not a foot patrol trying to lure them in.

VARGAS HELPED THEM CONCEAL the boat in a deserted tangle of mangroves that fringed the narrow beach.

Estrada's man was tall and sinewy with tight ringlets of steel gray that thinned on top. He exuded a calm assurance and professionalism that betrayed none of the tension he must have felt for living here so long under an assumed identity.

His truck, a twenty-five-year-old Chevy held together with baling wire, was hidden in some tall bushes near the dirt track that led to the Santiago road.

"Can't move before daylight," Felix warned them. "It would be inviting trouble, even if it is a holiday."

"What holiday?" asked Bolan.

"The Celebration of Socialist Brotherhood," Felix replied with a solemn face and cynical twinkle in his eye. He spoke English with a surprisingly refined British accent. In the years before the revolution his family had worked on the estate of an expatriate actor. His speech was punctuated with fluid gestures of his well-worn but delicately shaped hands. "There's a big parade in Camagüey. Out here, nothing much but fireworks...."

Bolan hefted the pack containing the C-4. He would make sure they got fireworks, all right.

The three men settled down to wait for dawn and the first stirrings of traffic on the main road. In whispered Spanish that was far too fast for Bolan to follow, Estrada outlined their mission for Felix, filling in the details that could not be included in the coded message beamed from Miami.

Vargas could add little to the information Estrada had assembled on the layout of Porcallo's headquarters.

"I can tell you his accommodations are in the same corner tower as his office. It's the one with all the radio antenna on top."

Bolan wanted to see this for himself.

"As soon as it's light, I'll drive you into the town," Felix promised. "I have a good excuse to visit Santiago. I always take some fish for Father Alfredo to eat on Fridays. He still likes to stick with the old traditions, says it's too late for him to change."

"The church remains open?"

"Yes, Father Alfredo still holds mass, but he's lucky if he gets a congregation of more than five or six people. Churchgoers are all noted by the CDR spies."

Felix Vargas was in contact with the Martinez family. He had been fishing with Eva's father. It was through them that he already knew of the plight of Julio Ortega.

Estrada's inside man was also aware of the American prisoner.

"Can you arrange for a meeting with Eva Martinez?" Bolan asked.

"Sure." Felix cocked his head. A car was passing. The high-pitched whine of its engine was too new and well tuned to have belonged to a local. "Russians. Probably going down to their private resort at Punta Julian."

"Are there many of them about?" Estrada asked his friend. "Do any of them have regular contact with Porcallo?"

"He gets an occasional visit from the KGB. My guess is that Russians don't want to reveal how much they really know about Porcallo's operation. The KGB's letting Fidel out on a long leash. They'll rap his knuckles fast enough when it suits them."

"For now, this dirty little scheme serves Soviet ends," Bolan agreed. "Who is the senior KGB officer in this sector?"

"Ratnikov. A weasel of a man. Stops every afternoon at Pilar—about ten miles on the other side of Santiago—to visit his whore, Esmeralda. He must like slumming with the field hands. Heavy girl, Ratnikov keeps her in a *bohio* on the edge of Pilar."

Estrada nodded toward the road. Two more vehicles were going past. "Time for us to join them."

"It'll be a smelly ride, I'm afraid," Vargas apologized, pulling back a square of canvas in the back of his truck. The box was laden with lobster traps and skeins of fishing net.

They climbed aboard and Vargas made sure the two raiders were completely hidden from view. He tugged his gear over the tarpaulin. "Next stop, Santiago del Este."

FELIX PARKED THE TRUCK in the small yard at the back of the church. Bolan and Estrada heard a muffled conversation with the priest before the canvas was drawn back. Bolan quickly scanned the surroundings.

The belfry stood empty. The bells had been removed, probably for the industrial effort, Bolan thought. But the tower remained intact. It was the best vantage point for a panoramic view of the port.

Father Alfredo, short of breath, led them up the steep wooden steps, then left them to their business. He sympathized with those who opposed the power of the atheistic authorities, but felt he was past taking an active role in the growing resistance.

Felix remained below to wait for Eva. The priest had assured them that every morning Eva came to light a candle and offer her prayers for Julio Ortega.

"Here," Estrada said, handing Bolan the lightweight Brunton binoculars.

The American blitzer scanned the harbor from right to left.

He focused on the drying sheds of the Camagüey Fishing Combine, then the tall mesh fence topped with barbed wire. Two guards stood duty at this outer barricade.

Bolan adjusted the glasses. The fortress came into view, backlit by the rays of the rising sun, its formidable walls glowing a sandy pink.

"See the radio masts?" Estrada asked.

Bolan had been inspecting the Soviet-donated patrol boat. Two deckhands were swabbing her down. It looked as if the sleek vessel had been out on a night run.

The image swept up past the massive wooden doors of the castle entrance and settled on the eavesdropping apparatus sprouting from the farthest tower. Bolan had no doubt which program the operators were tuned in on.

There was a creak on the narrow steps. Estrada, gun at the ready, opened the trapdoor. The frightened eyes of a pretty young woman peered up at him. He offered her his hand.

"This is Señorita Eva Martinez," said Felix. "She had come to pray for the prisoners of Carlos Porcallo."

"It does not matter what those pigs think of me. I defy them," she explained. "The man I love is already imprisoned for so-called antirevolutionary activities."

"I know why Julio was really slung in that hellhole," replied Bolan. "We're here to do something about it."

He showed her Estrada's diagram. The sketch was correct. Eva was able to add a few more details. "The stone staircase leading up to the commandant's office is here beyond the enclosure."

There were five other prisoners currently being held at Santiago. Porcallo had twenty militia serving under him, plus the crew of the patrol boat; they were billeted in the first barracks. Three officers were quartered in the other building.

Item by item Bolan built up a complete picture of Porcallo's fortress.

Their lives were going to depend on it.

"When will you next be allowed to see him?"

"There will be a visiting period later this afternoon," Eva replied, smiling. "Porcallo is displaying his compassion for the holiday."

Bolan nodded in satisfaction, He had gambled on the visiting time since Felix had first mentioned the Socialist Brotherhood Day.

"Look, I don't think we could fight our way down to the cells and back out again. Julio must met us halfway. How tight is the security on visiting days? How well do they search you?"

"Not much, *señor*. They look in my basket, of course. But this is not a proper prison, not like the big one in Camagüey. They do not have the facilities to strip us and..."

Eva did not go into the details of a body search; she was too embarrassed at the thought.

The sound of the villagers passing by the church to make ready for the later celebrations covered her momentary confusion. "Hector Alonso will be the guard on the gate today," she continued. "He's just interested in stealing the cigarettes I take for Julio."

The Executioner's thoughts were racing. Smuggling a gun inside was out of the question.

He opened the pack and extracted a tightly coiled length of braided steel and a small tablet of the puttylike C-4.

"Could you get this garrote and the explosive past the inspection point?"

He did not have to spell it out for her.

"*Sí, señor*, I think so. I could hide it in the one place..." Eva lowered her head, covering her blushing cheeks with the edge of her shawl.

Bolan squeezed her hand.

He told her exactly what she must instruct Julio to do, then made her repeat it. The slim fuse would have to be mixed up with some cosmetics in her bag.

Bolan turned to Felix, handing him a wad of folded currency. "Can you make sure that the people of Santiago put on the biggest fireworks display they've ever enjoyed?''

Felix took the money. ''You can count on it!''

''Okay, after you've set that up I want you to meet Eva and take her back to our boat. Now listen carefully. If Estrada and I are not back there by eight o'clock, you are not to wait. Not for a second, you understand? Shove off, use the RDF, and get out to the *Alicia*.''

Estrada could contain himself no longer. ''But what about us, *amigo*? What is your plan of attack?''

Bolan shook his head. ''We're not going to attack that place,'' he replied. ''We are going to drive right through the front gate.''

The Cuban raised an eyebrow at the fearless American's bold suggestion.

''Open up! I'm in a hurry,'' Bolan snapped in coarse but fluent Russian.

Estrada clapped him on the shoulder. He was grinning from ear to ear.

18

Felix Vargas trucked them to the outskirts of Pilar, then left. They passed Esmeralda's shack, well isolated from the other villagers, then Bolan and Estrada dismounted and crept back under cover of the tall sugarcanes.

There was a shed, housing an East German cutting machine, which gave them a good view down the dirt lane leading to the lonely *bohio*.

It was a one-room shanty, crudely built from rough planks and packing-case plywood, with a thatched roof and no running water or electricity. And, as Bolan noted through the glasses, there was no telephone hookup.

In most parts of Cuba the poorest families, often with seven or eight children, still lived in these pitiful huts despite all of Castro's grandiose promises of better housing for the masses.

Esmeralda lived there alone, ostracized from her people by her profession and her choice of clients. No one liked the Russians.

What pleasure Comrade Ratnikov derived from this peculiar arrangement was beyond Bolan's imagination. Perhaps it gave the KGB officer a sense of superiority over the Third World peasants. Bolan had learned the Russians' language, not what made them tick.

Forty minutes passed before Ratnikov arrived. Bolan spotted the thin dust cloud approaching through fields deserted for the holiday. "Paydirt," he said.

The dark blue Lada drove past them and pulled up about a hundred yards short of the *bohio*. Ratnikov obviously had his driver wait for him at a discreet distance.

The Cuban chauffeur, a young G-2 recruit who acted as full-time driver/translator, got out first, then he opened the rear door for the Soviet officer.

Bolan watched his pinched features through the binoculars as the tall thin Ratnikov tugged at the front of his tunic. Carrying a bottle of vodka in one hand, he walked up to the hovel. Estrada nudged Bolan. Esmeralda had appeared, and he wanted a look.

"Maybe he gets off on women weight lifters as well," whispered Estrada, stifling the urge to chuckle.

With carmine lipstick and vivid eyeshadow Esmeralda seemed like nothing less than a pathetic circus face painted on a bloated doll.

"We'll give him five minutes to knock back a couple of shots of vodka and get undressed, then we'll move in."

They waited.

The driver fished out a rag and began to dust off the chrome. Footsteps on the dirt road made him look up. A sugarcane worker was ambling down the track.

Estrada felt uncomfortable in the Gold Brigade T-shirt Felix had borrowed for him in Santiago. It was at least a size too small. He jerked his head in the direction of the tin shed.

"Just checking on our cutter! You know, we've had subversives disrupting things around here."

Ratnikov's driver looked visibly relieved. Subversion he understood. He liked kicking the shit out of those troublemakers. This guy was just doing his revolutionary duty.

"Hey, *compadre*, that's some car!" Estrada looked truly respectful.

He was only a couple of paces away when Bolan showed himself from the sugarcane. The driver swung around, startled by the sight of an armed man—a gringo!

Even as he opened his mouth to shout, Estrada shut it again with a devastating uppercut, followed through with a right to the stomach.

The young police recruit sagged against the Lada's trunk and slowly slumped forward. Estrada helped him with a chop to the neck and the man collapsed behind the car. Within moments he was bound, gagged and bundled into the front seat.

They approached the weathered *bohio* from opposite ends. Woven shades kept out the worst of the dust and the fierce afternoon sunlight; they also shielded Bolan and Estrada from view until they stood on either side of the doorway

It was a flimsy door and ajar but Bolan kicked it in for effect and swept into the room, a submachine gun in each hand.

Ratnikov was obliviously struggling toward his climax, enveloped by the copious flesh of his Cuban whore.

Esmeralda's eyes bulged with terror at the sudden appearance of the awesome apparition. For a fraction of a second, the Russian thought he had finally brought her to orgasm, then...

"Get your pants on, Colonel, we're going for a ride!" Bolan's Russian was crude, simple and direct.

Utterly deflated, outraged and more than a little frightened, Ratnikov struggled to obey.

Bolan scooped up the colonel's pistol belt. He did not wait for him to don his tunic. "Get out to the car. Move it!"

Estrada stepped across to where Esmeralda still lay panting on the disheveled bed. He pressed the cold muzzle of his pistol against the soft bag under her right eye.

"One word and you're dead."

She nodded mutely.

He poured out the vodka until the bedside tumbler was full to the brim. "Here, drink this...then sleep it off."

Esmeralda clutched the glass in trembling hands as she slurped it down. She needed a drink badly after what had happened.

Estrada ran out of the miserable *bohio*.

Ratnikov was shaking with a convulsive mixture of fear and anger. "Does the CIA never tire of playing its stupid games in Cuba? You shall not—"

"We're not with the CIA," Bolan cut off his empty threat. Neither the snub-nosed SMGs nor the Executioner's ice-blue eyes wavered for an instant. "And this isn't a game."

Estrada was driving. Ratnikov's chauffeur groaned in his struggle for consciousness. Bolan was watching the road past the Russian's shoulder. "That's the track Felix pointed out."

The Lada vanished into the waving stalks, following an old cart track that wound upward through the low hills between Pilar and Santiago. Some areas had been burned and slashed. The combine had already harvested as much cane as they were taking from this backcountry. It would be quite a while before anyone came through here again.

"Stop by that ravine ahead," said Bolan.

Estrada dragged the dazed recruit from the front. Bolan prodded the KGB colonel out of the car.

"Now you can take your clothes off again. That's right, all of them!"

Ratnikov paused, his trousers around his ankles. He seemed more concerned with his tattered dignity, being left stranded here naked in an alien land, than with the likely prospect of being shot. In fact, a bullet would have been preferable. "You are not going to..."

"Shoot you? No." It was not Bolan's way to kill a prisoner he had already disarmed. "Okay, stand still, my partner's going to tie you two up together."

Estrada slipped a noose around the colonel's neck. He would choke himself to death before he could free his wrists.

"You've got bad skin, comrade. A little sunlight will be good for it."

The Cuban patriot gathered together the clothes and dumped them in the car.

They were a few minutes behind schedule.

JULIO ORTEGA COULD HARDLY SUPPRESS his excitement as he was herded back into the cell after the visiting period. Only when he was sure the sentry had retreated to the outer corridor did he unbutton his shirt and show Paul Canfield what Eva had brought them. The young American was dumbfounded.

Ortega and Canfield had shared their confinement through the sullen silence of black depression and moments of grim humor when even the most trivial matters became the subject for life-sustaining laughter.

The Cuban hostage had taught Paul reasonably fluent Spanish; in exchange, the would-be adventurer had coached Julio in English with a Boston nasality.

"We have to make our move tonight at seven, as soon as they change guards." He tried to piece together exactly what was happening from what Eva had told him.

He did not tell Paul how she had smuggled the stuff through the visitor checkpoint. "Maria must have hired an American to bust me out. I told you my sister wouldn't let me down."

Canfield did not disagree with his cell mate. Privately he felt it far more likely that his father had found a mercenary—probably ex-CIA—to rescue him, and this guy had used Eva Martinez as the only available conduit. What the hell did it matter? For the first time they really stood a chance of breaking out.

They had practiced together for this very moment, hoping that one day they could fashion a model gun. Now they would have to do it with the tools miraculously at hand.

"Okay, go over everything she told you again. Is there anything you could have forgotten?"

FRIGHTENED VILLAGERS, chickens and a mangy dog scattered out of the way of the speeding Lada. Bolan, dressed as a KGB colonel, glanced out the rear window. One of the farmhands spat in the dust behind them.

The early-evening air was mild and fragrant. Estrada was sweating. He hoped no one would hear his heart thumping against his chest as loudly as the blood seemed to be pounding in his ears.

"Take it easy, *amigo*," Bolan steadied him. "Remember, we have the power."

Estrada drove through the main plaza of Santiago and followed the road rimming the harbor. The townsfolk were drifting in family groups toward the People's Park for the fireworks display.

He began to slow as they passed the fish sheds. The first barricade loomed in front of them.

The sentry straightened and moved forward, signaling for them to stop.

"Is Captain Porcallo in his quarters?" Estrada called out.

Bolan leaned to the window and waved his ID card impatiently. "Open up! I'm in a hurry."

Estrada did not have to translate the guttural order. The soldier tipped the counterbalance and the pole tilted up.

"Stop!" Bolan rapped his driver on the shoulder. "Ask that man when he last cleaned his rifle."

The sentry stood transfixed by the Russian's frozen glare.

"What if the Americans landed here? You must never relax your vigilance, you understand?"

Estrada bellowed out a translation. The soldier tried to stutter an apology, but the Lada swept past him.

The guard at the main gate had seen his comrade get a dressing down. He had the big wooden door half-open before the foreign car drew up.

Again Bolan flashed the stolen identity papers too quickly for proper scrutiny. "We're here to see Captain Porcallo."

The sentry was too startled to do anything but nod dumbly. He had just come on duty, hoping for a quiet evening on the waterfront so that he could watch the fireworks across the bay. Now some big-shot *ruso* had arrived. He knew Porcallo was always in a foul mood after the Russians came snooping around.

Estrada drove into the main yard unchallenged.

"HEY, DAVALOS!" Julio Ortega summoned the guard, his voice cracking with urgency. "Come quickly!"

The soldier glanced in through the bars of the outer gate. All he could see was Ortega signaling frantically through the small grille inset in his cell door.

"What the hell do you want?"

"It's Paul. He's ill! Real sick. It's that slop you feed us."

Davalos shrugged.

Come on, you bastard, we haven't got much time.

"You want the *yanqui* to die?" He probed for a nerve. "You want to explain that to Porcallo?"

The jailer reluctantly opened the gate and carefully locked it behind him, then, cradling his rifle, he stepped up to the cell.

Canfield gave a convincing groan. It did sound like a gut-wrenching attack of food poisoning.

Davalos peered through the barred opening. The American prisoner lay with his blanket twisted around his body. His face was dripping with sweat. He gave another awful moan and rolled his eyes piteously.

The Cuban soldier opened the door, warily motioning for Julio to stand well clear.

"He needs help...a real doctor," insisted Julio.

Davalos crossed to the cot to judge for himself. The young American certainly looked ill. Limp strands of blond hair were plastered across his damp forehead. As the guard bent forward to inspect Canfield, the other prisoner moved out from his corner.

"I told you to stand back, Ortega." Davalos looked up, poking with his rifle to order the Cuban back against the wall.

At the same moment he glanced away from Canfield, the American's hands shot out from beneath the blanket to loop the hidden garrote around their captor's neck.

Ortega sprang forward, unleashing a clasped-hand blow at the man's kidneys. Davalos fell. The wire cut through his larynx and strangled the warning scream in his throat.

"Get that rifle!" gasped Canfield. Ortega grabbed the weapon and snatched the keys from the jailer's belt. His cell mate pulled the wire tight with all the fury and resentment of his incarceration.

"Leave him, Paul. He's dead!" Julio restrained his friend. "Let's get the others."

They both ducked into the short passageway that led to the holding cells. Five astonished and grateful prisoners soon swelled their ranks.

It took three attempts to find the right key to open the barred entrance to the outer corridor. At the end of the dank stone tunnel were twelve steps leading up to a stout door opening into the compound. It was locked from the outside and guarded by another soldier in the courtyard stairwell.

"He's in for a big surprise," Julio whispered as he packed the malleable explosive into the lock and hinges.

Paul Canfield hoped his buddy had got the instructions right...or they would be the ones in for a nasty shock.

THE LADA PULLED UP across from the barracks. A sailor sat in the open doorway, polishing his boots in readiness for an evening's shore leave. Some of the other men were sprucing themselves up for a night on the town.

"Stick close to the car," Bolan whispered. "And keep those huts covered."

He looked up as he climbed out and saw a guard appear on the stone walkway outside the commandant's office.

The sentry was immediately followed by Porcallo himself, evidently forewarned of the Russian's arrival. He did not come running down the steps to greet this visitor. The captain asserted his true rank and importance by waiting for the colonel to come up to him.

Bolan took his time collecting the briefcase from the back seat. He had noticed there were armed men posted at each intersection of the surrounding walls. Through the mesh enclosure to his left he could see that a buttress partially obscured the short flight leading down to the dungeon door.

He checked his watch in the act of straightening the borrowed uniform. It was ten after seven.

Clasping the leather satchel in folded hands across his front, Bolan moved casually to the far end of the yard. He had traced back a violent trail of bribery, bloodshed and bullets to reach this lair, now he could afford no mistakes.

Porcallo looked down, watching his every step, wondering what the KGB wanted this time.

Bolan had taken three paces up when the first rocket burst with a glittering pop over the harbor.

One of the sailors called out to his friends, "Hey, they've started already. Let's go, you guys."

The impostor mounted the rutted stone stairway.

There was a flagstone walk running twenty yards to the door where Porcallo waited. He had covered half this distance when over in the park a second rocket whistled skyward—a real screamer this time—cracking apart into a fiery blossom of silver streaks.

A moment later it was followed by a second explosion—but closer, within the castle itself.

19

Porcallo started foward, pushing past the sentry with a puzzled frown. Something was wrong! He would not be fooled.

The captain was a big, heavyset man, but still he sprinted for the stairs, coming straight at Bolan.

Bolan politely stepped to one side, squeezing himself against the railing. But at the last moment, he stuck out his foot. It was all that was needed to send Porcallo flying. He had to grab for a stanchion with both hands to stop himself from tumbling into the yard.

The Russian visitor dropped the briefcase—just as he dropped all pretense as to his real purpose—and to the captain's guard it seemed as if the Jati just leaped into the stranger's hands.

The American hellfighter nailed the sentry to the door with a 3-shot burst through the chest. Then, seeing a startled face in the office window, Bolan tracked right and shattered it with another pull of the trigger.

The Cubans were taken completely off guard. A surprise attack had been launched from within the fortress itself.

At the sound of the dungeon door being blown open, Estrada had pulled a grenade from the car and lobbed it over the sailor's shoulder into the barracks corridor. A second MU-50 bounced into the troops' quarters before the first one had even gone off.

The sailor leaped to his feet, only to be hurled across the yard by the double explosion that shredded his companions with a lacerating barrage of steel pellets.

Estrada took cover behind the car while three of the militia escaped the writhing, screaming carnage through a door at the rear of the hut.

Bolan's full attention was on the walls. In short controlled bursts he was eliminating the sentries.

One of the topside guards crashed over into the exercise pen. Canfield darted forward and seized the fallen man's weapon.

A window in the officer's hut was smashed out with the snout of a pistol. The patrol-boat captain had an angle on the Lada—the treacherous driver was in his sights.

A rifle opened up behind Estrada, pumping rapid rounds into the broken window. Paul Canfield, once a crack shot in ROTC, put paid to any cross-fire attempt.

Julio blew the lock off the pen gate and ran to the car to give Estrada some needed backup.

Searing grenades and muzzle-flashes lit the darkened yard with flickering, demonic shadows as the survivors of the barracks tried to stave off the assault of the liberated prisoners. Neither side would show mercy.

The crackling, smoky, yelling melee in the courtyard was echoed in counterpoint by the cascading brilliance of the fireworks filling the sky over Santiago.

Porcallo, no longer dazed by his tumble, pulled the pistol from his holster.

Bolan twisted around and with one burst shattered the captain's knee, the second mangled his gun hand.

"No! Not until I've got the answers!" Bolan dragged the bleeding hulk of the Cuban chief the last twenty feet up to the office doorway.

Bullets chipped the stones above Bolan's head. The militiaman on the opposite tower hesitated to fire again, suddenly fearful of hitting the commandant. He should not have wavered.

The invader's death-spitting reply spun him in a death dance along the parapet, then he vanished from sight, dropping over the outer wall.

Porcallo's nerve center was filled with drab office furniture, except for a gleaming bank of the latest radio equipment.

The operator, who had somehow survived Bolan's fusillade, was groping around blindly, trying to set alight the papers he had stuffed into a metal wastebasket. The man's face had been ripped apart by the flying glass; the tattered flesh was a shiny wet mask of crimson horror.

Bolan fired from the hip. Bone, hair and brains splattered across the burnished control panels of the receiving equipment.

A burning match had dropped into the paperwork. Bolan jumped forward to save the evidence.

Porcallo was stretching upward, reaching with his good hand for a rifle from the wall rack.

Estrasda shot him from the open doorway. Three times. Head, chest and stomach. Porcallo subsided to the floor of his office, his face smashing down into a puddle of his own blood.

"Come on, Mack, quickly! The guards outside have shut the main entrance. We're bottled up in here!"

Bolan bundled the paperwork into the briefcase. Estrada tossed a last grenade back through the door. The Cuban listening station detonated in a flaming roar.

Ortega, Canfield and their fellow prisoners had complete control of the yard. An injured man inside one of the huts was still groaning for his mother.

"Turn the car around," Bolan ordered. He rigged the explosive pack while the freedom fighter reversed the Lada.

"I'll do it," volunteered one of the prisoners. Aiming straight for the big gate, the man threw himself clear at the last moment, rolling for cover behind the corpse of a guard.

The front entrance erupted in a deafening blizzard of splintered wood. The rescued men and the raiders spilled out with guns blazing.

"The boat!" Bolan shouted.

Paul Canfield was the first to jump aboard. The solitary sailor on watch had dived into the harbor and was swimming for his life. One of the vengeful Cubans shot him like a rat in a barrel. Canfield had the engines fired before the last man leaped onto the deck.

"I know these waters. I can pilot us through the reef," one of the prisoners said. He took over the wheel.

"Cast off!" Bolan called out, finding himself in command of a fully operational Cuban gunboat. Two of the men he had helped free acted as deckhands; a third was hauling up ammo for the twin fifties.

Spouts of water chased toward them across the inlet, small clouds of grit were spurting from the edge of the quay, whining ricochets bounced off the fortress walls.

"Russians!" Estrada yelled. He pointed back down the approach road.

A Jeep with rear gunner in action was leading two truckloads of Soviet personnel at full charge along the dockside.

"Ratnikov! Someone must have found him." Bolan ran for the machine gun. "Tell the helmsman to circle the harbor."

Churning up creamy billows of foam, the patrol boat sped away from its mooring. With the wheel hard over, she heeled in a tight turn to port. The last of the fireworks' tinsel showers was reflected on the mirrored surface as the vessel knifed its way toward the fishing jetties. Still circling, the pilot brought the boat around until it was racing alongside the road to the fortress.

Bolan raked the Russian convoy with a shattering broadside.

Tracers set fire to the old woodwork of the drying sheds.

The lead car, its driver dead at the wheel, slued sideways and exploded as it was rammed from behind by a truck. The third driver tried to avoid the flaming wreckage and managed to plunge headlong into the bay.

A loud cheer went up from the men aboard the boat as it ran for the narrow harbor entrance and the dark sea beyond.

Bolan poured one last volley through the smoldering entrance to Porcallo's headquarters and surveyed the inferno he had ignited.

"The Russians should be pleased to see their foreign aid is being put to work."

Felix Vargas was waiting to welcome them back aboard the *Alicia*. In fact, it was only his reading of Estrada's frantic signal that had convinced Ramon the gunboat was in friendly hands.

Eva greeted Julio with shining eyes and open arms. The young Cuban scarcely paid any attention as his companions scuttled the patrol boat. It was sent to the bottom of the Caribbean. One less disruption in an already overheated trouble spot.

"Castro will have to blame its loss on an inexperienced crew," Bolan said, "or explain to the Kremlin what the hell was really going on in Santiago del Este. And I don't think he'll want to face that."

"What about those Russians you wasted?" Estrada asked.

"A CIA-backed raid?" Canfield suggested. He looked knowingly at the man who had pulled him out of Porcallo's dungeons. "They'll make a complaint, then drop it."

He was still charged up with the raw excitement of that last thunderous, flame-spitting run from the harbor.

These older men were calm and collected, already planning for what lay ahead. Paul knew he was not cut out to be the rough, tough adventurer he had once dreamed of becoming.

Bolan was still staring coolly past Estrada at Canfield. And the Executioner couldn't help thinking of his brother, Johnny, and youthful enthusiasm. "You helped us out, kid, I'll grant you that, but I think you're out of your league. Go home, get a job or something." Bolan kept his voice deliberately gruff. Then he addressed the others. "Okay, let's check those papers."

The Cuban escapees were joking with the Santos brothers. Julio stood at the railing with his arm around Eva's shoulders as they watched their island merging into blackness off the port quarter. Canfield followed the two leaders down the cabin steps.

Bolan and Estrada spread out the papers that the Executioner had rescued from the wastebasket. Canfield sat quietly on the far side, trying to be as inconspicuous as he felt.

Bolan looked across at him. "You're still in deep trouble."

"I know. I'm willing to face the consequences...back *home*."

"Are you willing to testify about everything you know about this Cuban connection?"

Canfield nodded.

"What do you think?" Bolan asked his flanker.

"I can hand him over to Lieutenant Wallace. Miami police. Straight as a die. He'll give Paul a fair shake."

Bolan glanced back at the youth. "We can't make any promises beyond that."

"I realize that. Thanks for everything."

"Tell me, if you had made that run, how would you have known where to land so as to avoid a welcoming committee from the DEA?"

"If my partners hadn't tried a stupid double cross, we were to have received instructions from the Cuban commander who delivered the payload. He was the one who knew how to get us through."

"So the information came straight from Porcallo." Bolan began to sift through the mass of scribbled notes.

He lit a cigarette and continued searching. Estrada mumbled translations of some of the messages. Little of it made sense in the context of drug smuggling.

Finally Bolan spotted something. "What's this? Yeah...those numbers?"

Estrada was puzzled. "Just a note on a biblical verse. A quotation the operator jotted down. It's Jeremiah 30, verse 23. " 'The whirlwind...goeth forth in fury...it shall fall with pain on the head of the wicked.' "

Even as Estrada read out the words, Bolan was replaying Don Edelman's tapes in his memory.

The numbers on that scrap were underlined in red.... That was it!

"Of course!" he exclaimed. "I've been looking for a reference to a complete fix. You know, two coordinates giving both latitude and longitude. They don't need it! The gulf shoreline itself is the longitude. All Angell has to do is read out a chosen passage as the latitude...wherever it intersects the coast is to be the next safe landing point."

"You mean these figures—thirty, twenty-three—are the fix?"

"Check it out." Bolan ran his finger around the Florida Panhandle. "See, that drop was to be made in the bay behind Fort Walton Beach."

"Bayou country up there," Estrada confirmed. "Perfect for a midnight run."

"It was so simple it was bound to work." Bolan was trying to remember everything he had heard on those tapes. "After getting the necessary information from Webber, Angell probably tipped the receivers with a prearranged signal like 'There's a message here...' or 'Listen carefully...' Then he just read out the coordinates as a biblical quote."

Bolan stared out of the porthole at the hissing sea. Did Magnus Angell believe in anything but money? Did he ever heed the words of the Good Book he so dirtily abused?

Bolan remembered parts of a sermon delivered long ago by an army chaplain.

He could not quote chapter and verse, but he was reasonably certain of the passage: "Cursed be he that doeth the work of the Lord deceitfully, and cursed be he that keepeth back his sword from blood."

Did Magnus Angell ever see the warning—a truth he could not escape—that was written so plainly?

He should have.

He really should.

Because a whirlwind was upon him.

The Executioner was coming, sword in hand, to write the final verse.

20

Peter Ziman's plans for the evening had been shot to hell. He was looking forward to a quiet supper with his companion Melvin, followed by a screening of the latest gay videos, while they snorted a gram of the best Colombian.

Bolan's sudden appearance had ruined everything.

Don Edelman's avenger stood between Ziman and his car. The agent turned, ready to flee the car park, looking wildly for some avenue of escape.

"You are scum," Bolan growled, "all of you. I'm going to finish what Don started. You, Leo Webber, Magnus Angell, you're all finished."

Ziman registered no surprise at the mention of Angell's name. He was still numb with the shock of this unexpected confrontation. "No.... No, Webber said—"

"He said what?" Bolan snarled, twisting the front of Ziman's jacket. "What did Webber tell you?"

"He said he was going to get you."

Bolan shook his head. "No, I'm going to get him. And his boss."

"You can't touch Webber. He's with the federal government." Ziman was recovering his poise. That last point had given this big bruiser pause to think. "And you'll never get near Magnus Angell. He's got a battery of lawyers. And anyway, since that last nutcase took a swing at him, he's always armed and under guard. Angell is beyond your reach."

"I'll find a way," Bolan said. But there were some doubts. He released Ziman from his grip.

"The smart thing, Mr. Bolan, is to go with the flow." Ziman rearranged his jacket. "Don't try to fight them. Make them pay all right, but make them pay you in cold, hard cash. There's more than enough to go around."

Bolan seemed really undecided now. His anger subsided as he grappled with Ziman's suggestion.

"I can arrange something." The agent sensed he was gaining the advantage. "They'll pay you well to get out of Florida and forget what you stumbled into down here."

"It'll cost them," Bolan said.

"They've got it. I tell you, these guys can make it worth your while. Look, just let me speak to them."

Bolan shook his head, still hesitant to trust a man who had fingered his own client for a hit. "Okay, I'll talk to Webber. But, it's got to be direct. One on one. I'll meet him alone.... No, not alone, I want you there, too."

"Sure, but where?"

"There's a shopping mall opposite the Palm Court Motel. It's on 41, outside Cypress Beach. I'll meet the two of you there in the parking lot, at the south end, tomorrow afternoon at three. Be there."

"You won't be sorry," Ziman said, thankful to get away at last. "I'm glad you've listened to reason."

Bolan hardly heard his parting comment. The Man from Blood was listening to his heart, his conscience, his sense of justice.

THE CYPRESS BEACH SHOPPING MALL was not particularly crowded. It did better business in the winter months, but at this time of the year, most people drove straight through from Sarasota to Fort Myers.

There were not enough cars in the lot to disguise the two vehicles that parked at the north end a few minutes before three.

Bolan watched them in his rearview mirror. They were probably the same guys Webber rounded up to raid Chirino's boatyard, he guessed, and all of them just as crooked as their chief.

Two of the men got out and pretended to check the tires. The driver of the other car walked along the front of the mall, pretending to inspect the mannequins. But Bolan knew he was really keeping his target under surveillance in the reflective glass.

They were slowly closing in....

His engine was ticking over, but Bolan did not move. It seemed they were willing to take the flak for shooting down a "suspect resisting arrest" rather than risk having a real troublemaker on the loose.

Webber and Ziman drove up exactly on the hour. The literary agent even gave Bolan a small nod of acknowledgment as they cruised in over the first of the speed bumps.

The Executioner glanced around, then deliberately looked back over his shoulder at the vehicles covering the north exit. Webber's car was still closing on him, rolling to a stop, when Bolan gunned his vehicle toward the highway. He took off so abruptly he almost stalled.

The other men ran back to start their cars, but Webber was the only one who stood a chance of catching him.

Bolan drove fast, spewing grit as he turned down the beach road. He had checked out the route twice earlier in the day. He was pushing eighty past the bird sanctuary when he spotted Webber coming out of the S bend about half a mile behind.

The big soldier gained the causeway approach, racing along the long, low bridge that led out to the fly-blown sandbanks of the outer beach.

A cluster of palm trees marked the end of the causeway. The road disappeared in an almost right-angled turn behind a thick wall of dusty shrubbery.

Bolan's internal clock was counting down—everything depended on split-second timing.

The seashore road was deserted. Bolan suddenly pulled on the hand brake. The rear wheels locked as he wrenched the steering wheel tight to the left. The car screeched into the rubber-scorching drift of a bootleg turn.

In little more than the width of a single lane, Bolan had totally reversed direction.

He trod on the accelerator and—now straddling the center line—streaked back toward the causeway bend.

Ahead of him Webber saw the fugitive's taillights winking as he slowed down for a blind curve. Then the car vanished.

Webber came through the turn as fast as he dared. Ziman, white knuckled with fear, braced himself against the dash. Neither of them had yet realized that they were the ones being suckered.

The road in front of them was blocked! Bolan was coming straight at them like a bullet.

There was no time for evasive action. Without thinking, Webber yanked the steering wheel hard right to escape the maniac who was almost on top of them.

They bounced over the shoulder at sixty, rocketed across the brown grass and struck a palm tree head-on.

The front fender collapsed and headlights shattered. The grille was smashed back into the radiator. Slivers of fractured metal were punched two inches deep into the tree trunk. The rad ruptured explosively. The hood crumpled, tore from its hinges and slammed into the windshield. The heavier sections of the vehicle assembly started to decelerate, throwing the rear wheels up from the dirt. Webber and Ziman were still traveling forward at more than fifty miles an hour.

Ziman, his limbs locked rigid in frozen terror, felt his joints snap at the elbows and knees.

The two men, screaming, still upright, were lifted from their seats. The steering wheel splayed open under Webber's unyielding grip. The edge of the sun visor smashed into the driver's forehead. His chest was only inches from the steering column.

The front end had disintegrated. The back of the car was still moving at thirty-two miles per hour. It began to tilt higher. The men had not yet even slowed down.

Webber felt the steering column punch through his rib cage. Ziman's head crashed through the cloudy spiderweb of broken windshield. Abrasive fragments of shattered glass and metal splinters scoured his features down to the bone.

The rear end smashed back into the ground. The whole frame was ripped loose as the body bolts sheared under the jolting impact.

The brake pedal snapped off.

Ziman was torn right out of his highly polished shoes.

The final force of impact energy twisted the car as if it had been squeezed by a giant hand. All the hinges popped.

Webber's skewered body drooped sideways from the driver's open door. Ziman, his neck broken, was jammed in an untidy bundle halfway through the windshield space.

It took less than eight-tenths of a second. A last, gasping hiss, the rattle of glass shards and torn metal as the wreckage settled.

And then...

Nothing.

Just an eerie silence.

IT TOOK BOLAN three hours to reach Alachalafaya. Hard to miss the place. There were billboards all the way to the highway exit. Some asked if you were ready to keep that "Appointment with the Lord." Others begged for donations to complete the new broadcasting complex.

Bolan turned on the car radio. The program, a rundown on the latest gospel releases, was punctuated with promos for that evening's television talk show.

Magnus Angell was reassuring the listening public just what a good time they were going to have hearing what the fascinating Reverend Billy Ray Jones had to say about wrestling with the devil.

Bolan drove slowly past the front gate. Every car was being stopped and the occupants scrutinized before they could enter.

The floodlit buildings beyond rose like interlocking crystals, topped with a slender white tower that supported a revolving star, shining high above the surrounding transmitters beaming out Angell's message.

The audience for the television show was directed to a separate parking lot. They obediently shuffled through a detector hoop before being admitted to the complex.

A partly paved road ringed the property line. Bolan followed the circuit past where the work crew had parked their graders, along the graveled track at the back of a clump of pine trees. He stopped the car behind a sprawling rhododendron bush.

Estrada had supplied him with all that was needed, but still every item had to be checked out. Bolan ran through the operation in his mind. Nothing could be left to chance. Whatever happened inside, he would have to make a very fast withdrawal.

The fence was the easy part.

Bolan left the car and walked to the rear of the buildings, taking cover in the boxlike assortment of massive air-conditioning units. He found the maintenance door, which led into a pipe-lined, cinder-block passageway. Calling upon his innate sense of direction, the death-shadow stalked through the twilit corridors toward the back of Studio B.

Whispered voices and a giggle warned Bolan to take cover. The featured vocalist of the evening—a brunette with a lacquered hairdo and too much eyeliner—was chatting with a security guard. She did not look as wholesome as on the television screen, slumped against the wall chewing gum and dragging on a cigarette, which was totally forbidden in the dressing rooms upstairs.

"I gotta go," she said. "Jeez, I'm on in three minutes."

She snickered again as the fellow groped her backside.

Bolan waited for the guard to butt out his own cigarette and start off again on his rounds, before he followed the soloist to the rear entrance of the big studio.

The red warning lights were glowing. The show was on the air.

Live, right.

But there was also death in the air this night.

Bolan brazenly walked through the insulated double doorway and mingled in the backstage shadows with milling stagehands, a waiting guest and a teenage gospel group. Anyone who got this far was not about to be checked by security. They were part of the show.

The crowd gave a big round of applause for a lively rendition of an old favorite. The evangelist launched into a pitch for more contributions.

The floor manager had the special guest waiting in the wings. "You just walk on and take a seat opposite Magnus."

Bolan was at his shoulder in an instant. He gripped the visiting preacher's upper arm and stopped him in his tracks. "Uh-uh, I'm on first!"

The man in black padded lightly across the brilliantly lit set and took his place.

"What the hell...! He's not Billy Ray Jones!" exclaimed the producer from the glass booth. He called up the floor manager over the intercom headset. "What's going on down there?"

The monitor showed Magnus Angell held in close shot for his final plea before the camera switched to the next introduction. It was policy to cut to the third camera only when the host finished announcing the guest's name. The producer's assistants looked up from the console. No one ordered a switch.

"Who is that guy?" the producer demanded.

Angell held up his hands to quiet the applause and glanced across with a smile of welcome for...

Their eyes locked on each other.

Each man knew the other for precisely what he was. There could be no mistake.

The corrupt evangelist could see the blue-white flame of retribution flickering in the depths of those ice-cold eyes. And in that stern face he recognized his own executioner had come at last.

Thousands of television viewers saw Angell's mask crack wide open. The smile disappeared, showing only a naked face of greed, the close-up of a monster who would hold on to his power and privilege and prestige whatever the cost.

The audience in the studio and in thousands of homes across the Southeast saw Angell reach inside his jacket and pull out a pearl-handled Walther.

They all heard him snarl, "Goddamn you!"

He should never have tried to outdraw Mack Bolan.

The camera was still focused on Angell, but the mikes picked up the words, "Too late. You've got an appointment with the Lord!"

A single shot, center forehead, snapped back Angell's head. He tottered, fired one wild shot into the floor and toppled over.

Bolan's gun arm tracked across and he blew out the unblinking eye of the television camera.

Pandemonium broke out in the producer's booth. The audience was in uproar, panicking to reach the exits.

Bolan left the stage, escaping in the confusion.

The job was done.

There would be no delays, no plea bargaining, no appeals, no bribery and no extortion to get Magnus Angell off the hook.

He had chosen to commit evil. And in doing so he had been his own judge and jury. From the very start the verdict was guilty.

The Executioner had carried out the sentence.

And that was final.

MORE ADVENTURE NEXT MONTH WITH

MACK BOLAN

#83 Missouri Deathwatch

Anatomy of a blood debt

A Mafia hit team is trying to gain control of
St. Louis. The Executioner is only too aware that
if the attack succeeds, it will be a major setback
in his everlasting war.

Mack Bolan returns to the Missouri killground
to settle an ancient blood debt. And the leader
of the hit crew and his Black Ace—one of the
brotherhood's assassination elite—are marked
for death.

1. How do you rate _____ ?

   (Please print book TITLE)

   1.6 ☐ excellent   .4 ☐ good   .2 ☐ not so good

   .5 ☐ very good   .3 ☐ fair   .1 ☐ poor

2. How likely are you to purchase another book in this series?

   2.1 ☐ definitely would purchase   .3 ☐ probably would not purchase

   .2 ☐ probably would purchase   .4 ☐ definitely would not purchase

3. How do you compare this book with similar books you usually read?

   3.1 ☐ far better than others   .4 ☐ not as good

   .2 ☐ better than others   .5 ☐ definitely not as good

   .3 ☐ about the same

4. Have you any additional comments about this book?

   _____ (4)

   _____ (6)

5. How did you *first* become aware of this book?

   8. ☐ read other books in series   11. ☐ friend's recommendation

   9. ☐ in-store display   12. ☐ ad inside other books

   10. ☐ TV, radio or magazine ad   13. ☐ other _____

   (please specify)

6. What *most* prompted you to buy this book?

   14. ☐ read other books in series   17. ☐ title   20. ☐ story outline on back

   15. ☐ friend's recommendation   18. ☐ author   21. ☐ read a few pages

   16. ☐ picture on cover   19. ☐ advertising   22. ☐ other _____

   (please specify)

7. Have you purchased any books from any of these series or by these authors in the past 12 months? Approximately how many?

	No. Purchased		No. Purchased
☐ Mack Bolan	(23) _____	☐ Clive Cussler	(49) _____
☐ Able Team	(25) _____	☐ Len Deighton	(51) _____
☐ Phoenix Force	(27) _____	☐ Ken Follet	(53) _____
☐ SOBs	(29) _____	☐ Colin Forbes	(55) _____
☐ Dagger	(31) _____	☐ Frederick Forsyth	(57) _____
☐ The Destroyer	(33) _____	☐ Adam Hall	(59) _____
☐ Death Merchant	(35) _____	☐ Jack Higgins	(61) _____
☐ Rat Bastards	(37) _____	☐ Gregory MacDonald	(63) _____
☐ Hawker	(39) _____	☐ John D. MacDonald	(65) _____
☐ Nick Carter	(41) _____	☐ Robert Ludlum	(67) _____
☐ The Survivalist	(43) _____	☐ Alistair MacLean	(69) _____
☐ Duncan Kyle	(45) _____	☐ John Gardner	(71) _____
☐ Stephen King	(47) _____	☐ Helen McInnes	(72) _____

8. On which date was this book purchased? (75) _____

9. Please indicate your age group and sex.

   77.1 ☐ Male   78.1 ☐ under 15   .3 ☐ 25-34   .5 ☐ 50-64

   .2 ☐ Female   .2 ☐ 15-24   .4 ☐ 35-49   .6 ☐ 65 or older

Thank you for completing and returning this questionnaire.

Printed in USA

NAME _____
　　　　(Please Print)

ADDRESS _____

CITY _____

ZIP CODE _____

BUSINESS REPLY MAIL

FIRST CLASS   PERMIT NO. 70   TEMPE, AZ.

POSTAGE WILL BE PAID BY ADDRESSEE

NATIONAL READER SURVEYS

2504 West Southern Avenue
Tempe, AZ   85282